JUST MYRTO

LAURIE GRAY

LUMINIS BOOKS

LUMINIS BOOKS
Published by Luminis Books
1950 East Greyhound Pass, #18, PMB 280
Carmel, Indiana, 46033, U.S.A.
Copyright © Socratic Parenting LLC, 2014

Hardcover: 978-1-935462-96-5
Paperback: 978-1-935462-97-2

Printed in the United States of America

10 9 8 7 6 5 4 3 2 1

LUMINIS BOOKS

Meaningful Books That Entertain

Advance Praise for *Just Myrto*:

"In this very original novel, Laurie Gray gives us a cast of characters to love, a historical setting to inhabit, and just enough philosophy to whet our appetites for more. A page-turning narrative woven with deep and substantial conversations, *Just Myrto* lingers in the mind long after the book is closed. I especially love the delicacy with which Laurie Gray imagines several central scenes, giving love and sex and death their importance in the story, while allowing Myrto a certain modesty in recounting her feelings about them. A beautiful story, beautifully told."
—Helen Frost, author of *The Braid*, *Crossing Stones*, and *Salt*

"The character of Myrto, as the second wife of Socrates, will surely imprint for good all those who discover her in this delightful book. As a young girl without a dowry, Myrto could easily have fallen between the cracks of ancient Greek society. Instead, when Socrates volunteers to take her as a second wife, Myrto undergoes an initiation, not just into wife- and mother-hood, but also into the life of an independent thinker. She becomes a woman of great spiritual power, especially after the death of her husband, when she chooses how to live without her beloved guide and husband."

"What I loved most about this book is how the author resists the temptation of the romantic master narrative. Myrto develops great strength as she learns to think for herself. In fact, I've never seen a better depiction of growth in a young woman—from vulnerability and anxiety to confidence and courage."

"Socrates and Plato, two of the other chief characters, are finely drawn also. Indeed, Socrates is the catalyst for the amazing growth of his young wife. His refusal to tell her what to do and to think and his probing questions have a transformative effect over time. She even finds a way to understand the famously difficult Xanthippe, Socrates' first wife."

"Along the way the reader picks up many facts of Greek life and history, but the research doesn't show on the surface. It's embedded and can be discovered just the way Socrates himself would have approved. Without discovery, learning is mere memorization. With it, learning lives in the place of the gods, the spirit."

"I highly recommend th s book to anyone interested in ancient Greek culture and in a riveting story of female empowerment."
—Shirley Hershey Showalter, author of *Blush: A Mennonite Girl Meets a Glittering World,* former president of Goshen College and former Vice President of the Fetzer Institute

"I totally enjoyed this book based on real facts of the little-known second wife of Socrates. Laurie uses her imagination and places us in a world that is very different from the one we live in today . . . what it was like to be an uneducated, unmarried, young woman with seemingly few choices in ancient Athens after her father dies and she is left penniless."

"In Myrto's exchanges with Socrates, Plato and other historical figures, we also learn that we are the wisest when we keep an open mind, ask questions, and listen to others. This was done through the lively and interesting dialog throughout the story."

"We grow with Myrto as she learns what is truly important—freedom of thought and the choice it gives you. I think today's young women need heroines like Myrto, who blossoms from a poor, frightened, insecure girl to an independent, free-thinking woman . . . and it's not through kowtowing to other's expectations, but listening to what is important to your heart, and having the courage to move forward."

"Although I am far from being a teenager, I continue to grow and could identify with Myrto's thirst for knowledge and discovering her own path. I can wholeheartedly recommend this book for teens who love history, want to understand ancient Greek culture, learn about the Socratic Method, and see life through the eyes of an historical figure of ancient times."
—DeShawn Wert, YourADDAnswers.com

"Laurie Gray does an admirable job of weaving the philosophical content of Plato's dialogues into a compelling story."
—Naomi Reshotko, author of *Socratic Virtue,* and Professor of Philosophy, University of Denver

"Teens—and adults—interested in ancient Greece from a social and intellectual perspective will find this novel richly rewarding, as will fans of biography and readers who appreciate a 'human face' for famous names. In addition, *Just Myrto* offers intriguing glimpses of women's lives in ancient Greece, a notoriously male-centered society; this novel should find a place in feminist literature. Laurie Gray has gracefully met several major challenges in writing this unusual book, and her readers will thank her for a horizon-broadening experience."
—Ella Marston, author of *The Compassionate Warrior* and *Santa Claus in Baghdad*

Praise for *Summer Sanctuary* by Laurie Gray, an Indiana Best Book Finalist and Moonbeam Gold Medalist:

"Skillful writing allows readers to experience Matthew's struggle with life questions, his own beliefs, his emotional growth, and his actions to help Dinah."
—Susan Shaver, *Library Media Connection*, Starred Review

"What a big-hearted story, told with affection and humor. I loved spending time with Matthew and his family and with Dinah, the girl who looks in from outside. Like Dinah, young readers will find a place of welcome and comfort, a true sanctuary, in the pages of this book. Like Matthew, they'll discover something important about friendship and independence."
—Helen Frost, Printz Honor Award-winning author of *Keesha's House*

"This is a wonderful book. Any writer wanting to create a work of fiction that is appealing and spiritually fulfilling for teens or young adults would do well to read this before embarking on their journey . . . This is the type of book a librarian loves to pull off the shelf and hand to a teen reader looking for something that is a fun read with a healthy message. I look forward to more work by this author."
—John R. Clark, *TCM Reviews*

"*Summer Sanctuary* is a beautifully written tale that should appeal to all ages. Laurie Gray captures the heart of what it is to be young, and her characters reflect that joy. Designated as an OUTSTANDING BOOK."
—Debbie Wiley, *Book Illuminations*

"*Summer Sanctuary* is a delightful, heart-warming and thought-provoking book."
—Sahar, *Blogcritics*

"Laurie Gray does a magnificent job with character development in *Summer Sanctuary*. This is a beautifully written tale that should appeal to all ages."
—*Debbie Wiley Book Reviews*

"This quiet, sweet book about friendship is a rare jewel."
—Lyn Seippel, *Bookloons*

"Matthew and Dinah's story is a beautiful and touching one. The story is a well-written one and describes some of the feelings that teenagers have about their family, and about what it means to be a friend."
—Monique Burkes, *BookPleasures.com*

"*Summer Sanctuary* is an excellent book from novelist Laurie Gray. Hopefully Gray will continue writing and providing quality literature for adolescents with wholesome themes."
—Margo Nauert (6th grade teacher), *BookTrends.org*

"Rich in literary allusions and humor, this novel overflows with music, poetry and science, all appealing to and suitable for middle grade readers. The book creates a safe place for tweens and teens to explore and appreciate their own experiences as well as the diverse experiences of others."
—Bianca Schulze, *The Children's Book Review*

Praise for *Maybe I Will* by Laurie Gray:

"In *Maybe I Will*, Laurie Gray writes about important topics that teens need to talk about, including sexual assault, friendship, and alcoholism or self-destructive behaviors that result from trauma. *Maybe I Will* may help some teens know they're not alone."
—Cheryl Rainfield, award-winning author of *Scars*, *Hunted*, and *Stained*

"Sandy is written so as to be readable as either male or female . . . and the note it hits at the end is hopeful without being unrealistic. A careful treatment of a difficult topic."
—*Kirkus Reviews*

"Gray draws from her professional experience with teens in this fast-moving and emotional story."
—*Publishers Weekly*

"Author Laurie Gray deals with a difficult topic in a thoughtful, nuanced, and realistic way. A pinch of humor and dash of Shakespeare add flavor to what otherwise might be an overly heavy stew. *Maybe I Will* belongs on teens' reading lists and bookshelves alongside classics of its type such as Laurie Halse Anderson's *Speak* and Cheryl Rainfield's *Scars*."
—Mike Mullin, award winning author of *Ashfall* and *Ashen Winter*

"*Maybe I Will* is a fantastic story that stirs reader emotions and shares a meaningful story. I would recommend it to teenagers who enjoy realistic fiction and books like *Speak*."
—*LitPik*

"*Maybe I Will* is an essential purchase for libraries with young adults requesting books like *13 Reasons Why* by Jay Asher, *The Rules of Survival* by Nancy Werlin, *Speak* by Laurie Halse Anderson, and *Stop Pretending: What Happened When My Big Sister Went Crazy* by Sonya Sones."
—Diane Kelly, *PracticallyParadise.org*

"[Her] experience and her talent as a writer enabled Gray to craft characters whose emotions, motivations, and reactions seem realistic and utterly believable. I would definitely recommend *Maybe I Will* for high school age readers . . ."
—Ross Brand, *TheTrades.com*

"This is an important book. Parents with pre-teens and/or teenagers—buy this book, read it yourself and then pass it along to them to read. I am a mother of a teenager myself and I know that often teens shut their ears and don't listen to a lot of the wisdom and advice we have to offer. Encourage them to read *Maybe I Will*. It covers a lot of vital, important information about sexual assault."
—*Growing Up Little*

"*Maybe I Will* should be read by every teenager and required reading in schools. It's as important as reading *April Raintree* was for me when I went to school. The nature of the book, and the discussions it can bring up are truly important for a young audience to understand. Read this book with a warning—you will cry, and it will affect you."
—*Naimeless*

For my Socratic husband and our wondrous child.

Introduction

JUST MYRTO IS a work of historical fiction set in Ancient Greece. The main characters were real people who lived in Athens around the turn of the 4th Century B.C.E. Readers may refer to the Glossary at the end of the book for more information on the people, places, literature and mythology referenced in the book.

Prologue

I HAVE A favorite dream. In it, my mother is a goddess. I live, eat and play on Mount Olympus with the gods. I have an endless supply of ambrosia to satisfy my hunger, and the nectar flows freely upon the slightest notion of thirst. I ride on Pegasus, the winged horse, with no fear of flying, no fear of falling and no fear of dying because the gods never die.

In this dream, I am free. I am not just Myrto, daughter of Lysimachus and granddaughter of Aristides the Just. I am an immortal soul, living and breathing eternally. The entire universe is my playground.

But then it never fails. As I soar through the white clouds, Pegasus vanishes. I feel myself falling. The clouds turn dark, and I disappear in the fog. I awaken to a memory of death and the misery that is my life. I was born into a world where life itself depends upon man's pleasure and woman's pain. I am doubly cursed to be both mortal and female.

Memories of my mother's death often awaken me at dawn. They drive me out of the house and up the hillside to a place where the virgin goddess Artemis decides the fate of abandoned baby girls. The hill is very near my home in Alopeke. From there I can see across the River Illisus to the wall surrounding Athens. I sit and watch the sun rise upon the temple of Athena in the Acropolis.

1

MY MOTHER DIED during the month of Poseidon in the winter of my twelfth year. I had just blossomed from girl to woman. I dedicated the clay toys of my youth to Artemis in anticipation of the wedding that was sure to follow. But there was no wedding for me. Instead, I watched my mother perish giving birth to a stillborn son.

The moment my mother's breath stopped, the midwife ripped her apart in haste to free the child. The midwife's wailing drew my father into the room. Father took my lifeless brother from the midwife and fell to his knees still holding the child. He stayed there, silently clinging to the infant corpse as the midwife cleansed the room of my mother's blood, washing away the remains of her life.

I saw no anger on Father's face. Bewilderment gradually changed to despair as the winds of truth fanned sparks of realization. He named the boy Acheron after the river to Hades, the final resting place of all mortal souls. At the time, I thought he meant to keep the dead child. I wondered which was the greater tragedy—a stillborn son or a live daughter who, having no mother to raise her, very likely would have been abandoned on the hillside. Was Father mourning the loss of a son more than the loss of a wife?

Father remained in a trance throughout Mother's burial preparations, funeral and cremation. Then the despair consumed him, eventually subsiding into the ashes of grief. He wanted nothing more than to have me near him as the life slowly drained from his aging body. Other girls my age, all betrothed to marry, left their homes one by one, but I spent each day at Father's side in the place that had been my mother's.

Every morning as I greeted him with a kiss Father would say things like, "Your beauty reminds me daily that the gods have been good to me despite my shortcomings. My father before me lived a life of greatness, but there is no greatness in me. May the greatness of my father, Aristides the Just, pass through my seed to your brothers."

There was never any talk of anything being passed on to me or any future for me apart from my father. My only dreams were those that came to me in my deepest sleep. My only hope was in the charity of the man to whom I belonged. As I rubbed olive oil into his leathery skin each day, he would often say, "Forgive me, Myrto. I am old and foolish. Perhaps I find too much pleasure in the fact that I have no dowry for you to marry."

In the evenings before dinner he frequently remarked, "You are such a comfort to me, my child. Your unfailing devotion brings me great joy."

And so the years of my full bloom passed. My older brother Nikomedes joined the military, and my younger brother Apollodorus became the apprentice of a prominent Athenian physician. Eventually, our oldest brother Aristides returned from battle. I had no life apart from caring for Father and no notion of what might become of me when Father died.

Shortly after my eighteenth birthday, Father summoned Aristides to his bedside. I remained in the room, though they discussed my future as if I were not there.

"Aristides," said Father, "The gods are calling. Apollo has certainly pulled an arrow for me from his quiver and drawn his bow. All that I have, though I know it's not much, belongs to you to do with as you will. Your marriage is already arranged to Charis following her fourteenth birthday. Nikomedes and Apollodorus will find their own way. My only request is that you find a worthy husband for Myrto."

"How am I to give her in marriage?" Aristides implored. "Who would take her without a dowry? It would take years to scrimp and save a reasonable sum. By then she'll be well into her twenties or thirties!"

"It's true I have no riches to offer with her," Father said sadly, shaking his head. "Aristides the Just was a brave soldier and much beloved statesman, but he never accepted wealth in exchange for serving Athens. I have given you his name and done my best to educate you in good citizenship, but I leave you little more than he left me."

"Father, what would you have me do?" asked Aristides.

"I have no answers," Father admitted. "Talk to Socrates, your boyhood teacher. The Oracle once declared him the wisest man alive. Ask Socrates."

And with that Apollo released the arrow that ended our father's life. I felt the warmth escape his body as I bathed him in rose water. I dressed him in his most festive white tunic and wound a crown of wooden ribbon and ivy around his forehead. I removed an obol from his coin purse and placed it in his mouth to pay the ferryman for the journey across the rivers Styx and Acheron into the Underworld. I prayed that Hermes would deliver Father safely to Hades to be reunited with his own more renowned father, Aristides the Just.

When Apollodorus arrived later that evening, he and Aristides laid Father out on a couch in the front courtyard. "Face him toward the door to greet the mourners," instructed Aristides.

Apollodorus complied. "Don't forget to set out the purifying water, Myrto," he said.

"I will do that now," I replied. I selected a tall earthen vase and placed it in front of our house. Then I grabbed two large buckets and walked to the river. By sunup the house would be full of mourners dressed in black for the gloomy vigil. Friends and relatives alike would moan and weep loudly as they entered. As they left the house, they would all sprinkle water on themselves to wash death from their bodies.

The cool night air filled my mind with questions. *What will become of me now? Will Aristides find me a suitable husband?* Other brothers might consider selling a sister who had no dowry into slavery, but surely Aristides would honor Father's dying wish to find me a husband. *Socrates will know the best way for Aristides to find me a husband.* I prayed to Athena that she would grant both Aristides and Socrates wisdom.

When I returned Aristides and Apollodorus were sitting in the courtyard. "Father is to be buried along the Street of Tombs next to our grandfather, Aristides the Just," said Aristides.

Apollodorus nodded. "He will need a tombstone."

"I've already made the necessary arrangements," replied Aristides.

"And the inscription?" asked Apollodorus.

"Lysimachus, son of Aristides the Just, farewell."

Tears filled my eyes. I carried a lamp back into my bedroom where I let down my long dark braids. *How long my hair has grown in six years.* I ran my fingers through the thick strands. *How well I remember the one and only night I cut it.* I sat fiercely brushing the memory of Mother's death out of my head. Then using a razor, for the second time in my life, I severed every flowing strand of hair in mourning.

2

ONE MORNING NOT long after Father's funeral, I awoke to see Aristides sitting beside the statue of Hermes in our courtyard. One of my earliest memories as a child was of Aristides sitting in that exact spot waiting for Socrates to arrive. Normally, Aristides would go to the Agora to find Socrates, but on this occasion, Father had invited Socrates to our home. Aristides sat poised with his wax-covered, wooden tablet and a narrow bone, chiseled to a point, desperate to write something that he could memorize and recite to please our father. Socrates engaged Aristides in a conversation that lasted all morning, but he never instructed Aristides to write a single word.

Now when Socrates arrived, Aristides jumped to his feet and practically shouted, "Good morning, Socrates!"

"Greetings, my young friend," Socrates replied. "I offer you my most sincere condolences on the passing of your father."

Aristides nodded and ushered Socrates to a wooden couch in the courtyard. They continued to pay their respects to Father, speaking well of the life he had lived.

Socrates looked exactly the same as a decade ago. Perhaps his gray beard was a bit longer, but his feet were still bare, and he wore the same weathered tunic. He was a curious old man, eyes full of laughter and lips full of questions. Was he really the wisest man of all? He didn't look at all like the judges and sophists I'd seen at Father's funeral. They seemed to take themselves and their wisdom more seriously.

I gathered a number of figs and dipped some crusty bread in wine for Aristides and Socrates to enjoy as they discussed my future. A pleasant taste in their mouths would surely result in a more pleasant life for me. *Please let them choose for me a husband who is kind. It is better to be slave to a kind master than the wife of a cruel husband.*

"So this is Myrto." Socrates smiled warmly as he said my name. I bowed my head and offered him the food I had prepared.

"She is already in her eighteenth year with no marriage prospects and no dowry," Aristides lamented. "What would you do if she were your daughter, Socrates?"

Socrates selected a fig. "Ah, but she is not my daughter, Aristides."

I could feel his eyes upon me, but I dared not let my eyes meet his. I placed the plate between them and backed away.

"Have you someone in mind who might accept her if she had a dowry?"

"No. Most of my friends are already married or betrothed. Others have died in battle. My mother has a brother who was recently widowed. He might agree to marry her out of family duty and the hope of having another healthy son or two."

"There you have it," said Socrates. "A perfectly good solution." He sampled a morsel of bread.

A perfectly good solution indeed! It was Uncle's abuse which fated our auntie to an early grave! I stepped back into the salon and perched by an open window. My flesh quaked and my blood swirled. I felt consumed by Poseidon himself. *Oh, Hera, goddess of marriage! Hear my prayer and intercede on my behalf. Anyone but Uncle!*

"I'm not so sure," pondered Aristides. "If that is what Father had intended he could have arranged that himself or instructed me to do so." Aristides reached over to the plate, grabbed a handful of figs and popped several in his mouth.

"True enough," agreed Socrates.

"But he did not," Aristides continued, shaking his head and chewing slowly. Finally, he swallowed. "Father instructed me to talk to you."

Socrates smiled and helped himself to a large portion of the wine-soaked bread. "A rather strange instruction, don't you think?" Socrates asked.

"I do. After all, you never really taught me anything," said Aristides. He furrowed his brow and stroked his shiny, black beard. "Still, when I was with you, I made tremendous progress in my education."

"Yes," mused Socrates. "I've often wondered how our lessons would have concluded had you not sailed away so abruptly on that military expedition."

Aristides began pacing about the courtyard. "And now that I've returned, and with Father's passing, it seems everything I ever learned has trickled away," he confided. Aristides stopped directly in front of Socrates and threw up his hands. "What should I do?"

"So far, you have considered only the widowed and the unmarried," said Socrates. "What about the Athenian decree that allows married men to take a second wife in hopes of replenishing the citizenry in these war-torn times?"

"An excellent suggestion!" Aristides sounded encouraged. "But she still has no dowry," he said, pacing once more. "Who will want another mouth to feed with no dowry to offer?"

"Dowries are not always such a good thing," countered Socrates. "Recall the dowry of the very first wife, Pandora. When her jar opened, all of the evils known to man flew out." He held out his arms as if offering Aristides a world of pain and suffering. Slowly, Socrates brought his hands back together and held them in an empty cup before Aristides. "Wouldn't you prefer nothing over a dowry of sorrows?"

"I would," agreed Aristides, "but I doubt that I can persuade another as easily as you've convinced me." Aristides studied Socrates from head to toe. "I can never tell if you are being serious or just playing with me," Aristides said, taking a seat beside him.

"My boy, I would never recommend for another that which I could not accept for myself," said Socrates. Aristides stared at Socrates with a look of puzzlement. All at once his whole face brightened.

"By Zeus, that's it!" exclaimed Aristides, jumping to his feet again. "Socrates, you must marry Myrto! What could be more suitable to Father and the gods than for the lineage of Aristides the Just to be joined with Socrates the Wise?"

I pushed the wooden shutter open and beheld Socrates with new eyes. I surveyed his rounded belly and short, hairy arms and legs. When I focused on his face, I saw only bulging eyes, big ears, fat lips and a large, pug nose. Socrates had absolutely no feature that one might call attractive.

I held my breath, expecting Socrates to laugh and dismiss Aristides' foolish notion. He did not. Instead, he sat quietly gazing at our terra cotta rooftop as if it were a stage; he appeared transfixed by the drama unfolding before him. Aristides did not seem troubled by this long silence. He finished all the figs and bread, then reclined on the grass near Socrates feet. Aristides' smile broadened with every passing moment he waited.

Finally, when the midday sun shone directly down upon them both, Socrates nodded suddenly, slapped his knees and announced, "Aristides, I am flattered by your kind offer. I accept."

"The gods will most certainly be pleased!" cried Aristides.

"I wish I could say the same for Xanthippe," replied Socrates. Everyone in Athens knew how exasperated Xanthippe was over the way her husband chose to conduct his affairs. What would she say about a second wife? "Then again, my old wife and my new wife may quickly conspire against me."

Aristides laughed. "You've always said that a good wife makes a man happy, but a bad wife makes a man a good philosopher. Whatever shall become of a philosopher with two wives?"

Socrates smiled. "We shall see soon enough. I'll make the necessary preparations at home. What would you like to do about a wedding?"

Aristides shook his head sadly. "We've exhausted our funds on Father's funeral. Anyway, a formal ceremony would only publicize Myrto's shame in having no dowry and sorrow in having no surviving parent to present her to you. A modest, private ceremony will be best."

Socrates nodded. "Very well. You may deliver my bride to my door tomorrow evening."

And so my fate was decided.

3

WHEN I AWOKE the next morning, I begged Pegasus to carry me back to sweet slumber, but to no avail. Instead, our slave Timo knocked and entered my chamber in a single motion.

"Bion and I have filled your mother's vessel with water from the river to give you your bridal bath," advised Timo.

Father had purchased Timo the month before Mother died to help care for the new child. He'd gotten a good price because Timo was heavy with child herself. When he presented her to Mother, Father said, "A slave for you, my love, and one for our child."

"But what if she dies in labor, Lysi?" Mother worried aloud.

"No matter," Father replied. "I'll find you another." Then he kissed mother's forehead and added, "But she won't. Everything is going to be fine."

Father was so right and so wrong. Timo did not die in labor, but everything was not fine. Several weeks after Mother's death, Timo's son Bion burst into the world oblivious to our sorrow. His rosy cheeks and curly locks exuded happiness regardless of circumstance.

"Timo, how can I marry Socrates today? There's been no feast and no sacrifice. The women of Alopeke will surely be offended that I've not called upon them to attend to my pre-wedding rituals. How will I ever face them?"

"I am sorry, miss." Timo sighed and held out my tunic. "What would you like for me to do?" She handed me my garter belt so that I could wrap it around my waist one last time.

I stared at the belt thinking of the young brides-to-be who chose to wrap that garter around their necks and hang themselves rather than allow an undesirable groom to remove and discard the belt forever. I closed my eyes and rejected the impulse to dishonor myself and my family. I focused my eyes on Timo as I put on the belt.

Timo had mothered me right along with Bion for the past six years. This morning of all mornings I wanted her to talk to me like a real mother, to give me the strength and courage to face this day. My only desire was to pull the covers over my head and fade into my dreams forever. *What do I want?*

"Would you please bring me the chamber pot?" I asked.

"Yes, miss." Timo nodded and fetched the shallow clay vessel and lid.

As I arose from my childhood bed for the last time, I realized that it was not the scorn of the village or the events of the day that I feared most. What would happen when the day was done and I lay down to sleep in Socrates' chambers? I shuddered.

"There seems to be a bit of a chill this morning," said Timo. "We'll warm your bath water for you."

"Thank you," I replied. I felt my chest and throat tighten, filling my eyes with tears. "I'm going to miss you, Timo."

"Thank you, miss. Bion and I will surely miss you and will offer prayers to Hera every day. Wife of Zeus and goddess of marriage, she will be with you always." Timo took my hand and wrapped me in my tunic for extra warmth. "Come now, miss. Your wedding is cause for great celebration, with or without a feast."

"Without. And without a dowry. And without my parents. Oh, Timo, this is not how I imagined it." I flung my body back on the bed, buried my face in my pillow and sobbed. The pillow eagerly absorbed my tears, but refused my sorrow.

"Nothing is ever really as good or as bad as we imagine, miss," Timo said trying to reassure me. "Apollo will ride his chariot across the sky tomorrow just as he's doing today."

There was no stopping Apollo's chariot. My thoughts returned to Socrates' empty hands as he spoke of Pandora's dowry. Not everything in Pandora's dowry was evil. After all of the plagues and pestilence had released, there—hidden beneath it all—was hope. Pandora at least brought hope into the world. But Socrates' hands remained empty. I would enter this marriage with no dowry and no hope.

I took a long, ceremonial bath. Timo anointed my body with scented oils, but I found no pleasure in the aroma. I cut two locks from my head of already short hair, leaving one amongst the flowers in the courtyard as a remembrance. The other I burnt as an offering to Artemis, praying that she would protect me and ease my passage to womanhood. I ate my last meal with Aristides and Apollodorus and packed my clothing and personal items.

Shortly before sundown, Timo placed my bridal veil on my head as Apollodorus prepared the cart for my departure. Epiktetos, who had been our slave for as long as I could remember, brought me a beautiful bouquet of myrtle, Aphrodite's favorite flower. Was it even possible that the goddess of love and sexual desire would accompany me to my new home?

Aristides took my hand and helped me into the wooden cart. "You are a beautiful bride, Myrto. I'm sorry we have no horse-drawn chariot to carry you away."

Hiding behind my veil, I didn't bother to force a smile. Instead, I nodded to reassure him. "I am grateful for a cart pulled by mules," I said, and it was true. Horses would only have carried me away more swiftly.

Our humble wedding party set out. Apollodorus joined Aristides and me in the cart and played wedding songs on his lyre. Timo and Epiktetos walked along beside us carrying torches to scare away Hades' spirits of death. Wearing a crown of thorns and nuts, Bion danced around in between Timo and Epiktetos, swinging a basket filled with the traditional bread, apples and flowers.

I rode silently, watching the half moon. The beat of the donkeys' hooves accentuated the sound of the cart's turning wheels along the dusty road. As darkness descended upon us, the others began chanting, *"Oh, Hymen! Oh, Hymenaeus!"* After several rounds of chanting, Apollodorus began to sing:

Hear this hymn to Thee, Oh, Hymen,
Holy God of Bride and Groom.
Make this marriage ever fruitful,
Many sons born from this womb.

Oh, Hymen! Oh, Hymenaeus!
Oh, Hymen! Oh, Hymenaeus!

Son of Muse and God Apollo,
Revel in this couple's love.
Join them in their consummation;

16

Send your blessings from above.

Oh, Hymen! Oh, Hymenaeus!
Oh, Hymen! Oh, Hymenaeus!

I bowed my head and closed my eyes the remainder of the journey. The cart lurched to a stop in front of Socrates' house. Socrates and his son Lamprocles greeted our wedding processional. I studied Lamprocles and guessed his age to be somewhere around 14 years. He did not look like a young Socrates, so I imagined he looked more like Xanthippe.

Bion danced his way over to Socrates and handed him a loaf of bread. His sweet young voice imparted the ceremonial words of prosperity and good luck: "I fled worse and found better." He giggled and danced back to his mother.

Socrates handed the bread to Lamprocles and performed the rite of grabbing my wrist and pulling me from childhood to adulthood. Since Father was deceased, Aristides declared solemnly, "In front of witnesses I give this girl to you for the production of legitimate children."

Socrates helped me out of the cart and lifted my bridal veil. I dared not look into his eyes. Instead, I watched Apollodorus as he poured a cup of wine for each of us. I searched the silver moon for a sign from the gods that I was to drink from this cup.

It is not too late. Artemis may yet shoot an arrow that whisks me off to Hades and restores me to my parents. I held my breath, but the gods did not intervene. Instead, Aristides offered a toast for our health, happiness and fertility, and I drank from the cup I was given.

4

AS THE MEAGER wedding party departed, Socrates led me into the house. Two small lamps on a table cast shadows across the room. Lamprocles picked one of them up and bade us good night. Socrates took the other one.

"The household has retired early this evening," said Socrates. He placed his hand on my shoulder and guided me back to his chambers. "You'll meet them all tomorrow."

I said nothing. An eternity existed between tonight and tomorrow. I stole shallow breaths from the air as we entered the room. I searched for anything familiar that might bring me comfort in my new home. The most dreadful fright possessed me as I beheld for the first time the bed of Socrates.

There was nothing frightful about the bed itself. It was larger than my own, but seemed smaller than the marital bed of my parents that I recalled from childhood—the bed where Mother died; the bed that Father burned.

Fear strangled my heart, and coldness passed through my limbs. I closed my eyes and imagined I was staring into the face of Medusa, hair of serpents, eyes that turned men to stone. *Change me to stone! Make me a rock! Do not revive me until this awful night has passed.*

"Please, make yourself comfortable." His voice was kind. *What trickery is this? Do not be fooled by the sweetness in his voice. I am a stone. Stones do not speak. Stones do not feel. Stones do not care.*

"Myrto, I mean you no harm." Socrates seated himself on one of the wooden chairs at the foot of the bed. *You mean me no harm; so you say. I suppose the spider means no harm to the fly. He merely wants his supper.*

"Come, have a seat." Socrates motioned to the other chair. "Are you hungry?"

I recognized Bion's basket on the low table between the chairs. The bread, fruit and flowers came from my own home. I kept my eyes on the basket and sat down.

"You've not spoken a word," said Socrates. "I want to hear your voice. I want to hear your thoughts. I want to see the world through your eyes."

I closed my eyelids firmly, damming a river of tears.

"Can you speak?"

I nodded, bewildered. *Yes, I can speak, but I have nothing to say.*

"Is there anything you'd like to tell me?"

I shook my head.

"Very well, then, my lovely Myrto, let the first word that passes from your lips to my ears be my name. Would you say it, please?" He waited.

"Socrates," I finally whispered.

"Delightful!" Socrates exclaimed. "Oh, please do say it again." Again he waited.

"Socrates." I spoke the word softly.

"Absolutely beautiful! And now, my dear, would you do me the honor of looking into my eyes as you say it?"

LAURIE GRAY

Slowly, I shifted my gaze from the basket to Socrates' countenance, keenly aware that I had never looked into any man's eyes other than Father's. Curiosity replaced a small portion of my fear. I felt my own eyes fill with tears as they met Socrates' eyes for the first time.

"Socrates," I said again, feeling as if I were seeing and being seen for the first time.

"Myrto," whispered Socrates. "My Myrto."

I began to tremble, not from fear, but overcome by a feeling of awe. Socrates eyes were very light brown—the color of my favorite goat when I was a child. I milked her every morning for years. On cold winter days, she would let me stroke her soft fur and rest my head against her side. Listening to her little heart beating, I found comfort in the warmth of her body. I scratched the top of her head until she bleated gratefully.

Then when I grasped the goat's teats between my fingers and pulled, the milk flowed so freely. The sound of the liquid streaming against the bottom of my metal pail always made my mouth water. When the bucket was full enough to please my mother, I aimed the teat directly toward my mouth. There was always enough sweet, warm milk left to satisfy my own belly.

I realized I was still gazing into Socrates' eyes, so warm and inviting were they.

"Did you see yourself?" Socrates asked.

I nodded, still holding his gaze.

"Excellent," whispered Socrates. "You know the eyes are windows to the soul. As I looked into your eyes, I saw the most beautiful, happy child."

I puzzled over this. Did he also see me? Did he see himself? Did he see the child he hoped to conceive?

20

"Myrto," said Socrates, taking my hand. "What is it you desire?"

No one but a slave had ever asked me this. *What do I desire? What have I asked for in the past? Food, water, a chamber pot. These are needs, not desires. Have I ever dared desire? Only in my dreams . . .*

My mind raced back to the wedding hymns and blessings. This was what I was supposed to say. "I desire what every woman desires," I said. "A son."

"Ah, yes," replied Socrates. "Sons are wonderful. I have a son." Socrates poured us each a cup of wine, raised his cup and waited for me to raise mine as well. "To sons."

With that desire in mind, I drank deeply from the cup. The wine was much stronger than I expected. In our home our wine was mixed with equal parts of water. Socrates' wine tasted uncut. I could feel it rushing into my stomach and swiftly making its way into the muscles of my neck and shoulders.

Socrates smiled and again raised his cup. "To sons!" Again we drank deeply. The wine danced down my back and into my legs. *How many cups of wine will it take for me to be ready for Socrates to try to give me a son?* I set my cup on the table and again found myself afraid to meet his gaze.

Socrates also set his cup down and gently lifted my chin with his hand, looking once again into my eyes.

"Myrto," he said. "Are you afraid?"

I felt my heart pounding, but the wine was loosening my tongue. "Should I be afraid, Socrates?" I examined his face for the answer.

Socrates tilted his head and appeared to give this serious consideration. Finally, he replied, "Fear is not about *shoulds* and *should nots*, Myrto. If and when you feel it, fear just is."

As he said these words, my fear evaporated.

"I will never force myself upon you, Myrto. If you desire a son, I am honored to attend to that desire at your request."

I hesitated, wondering if I could believe my new husband. "But my brother has given me to you for the production of legitimate children regardless of my desire," I said.

"I made that contract with your brother, it's true," conceded Socrates. "But your brother is not here. Now that you are my wife, are we not free to make our own covenants?"

Surely he is mocking me. Men make agreements with men, not women. No contract with a woman can be binding. "You would make an agreement with a woman?" I asked.

"Most certainly," Socrates said nodding, "but even more importantly, how can I be sure that you are a woman and not a goddess in disguise?"

I laughed aloud. "The wine is playing tricks upon us both!" I poured more wine in both our cups and raised my glass. "To the wine!"

Socrates raised his cup, but took only a sip before setting it back down on the table. "Would it not be just like Pallas Athena to disguise herself as the granddaughter of Aristides the Just to see if I would indeed treat her justly? Or Aphrodite to appear in the form of a beautiful young woman named after her favorite flower?"

Socrates took the wine from my hand, set it on the table and took both of my hands in his. "My flesh is mortal, my dear Myrto. I have learned to allow a goddess to express her desire rather than impose my own desires upon her. No mortal man can dominate a goddess and hope to survive."

He kissed my cheek and led me to the bed. "Come," he said. "Let us sleep. Tomorrow you can think again about what it is you desire."

22

5

THE NEXT MORNING the fear of living in Xanthippe's house replaced my fear of sleeping in Socrates' bed. I awoke to distant sounds of her ranting. Xanthippe means "yellow horse." I pictured her reared up on her hind legs, neighing loudly and knocking me to the ground with her powerful front hooves. *Perhaps it would be best for me to stay right here until Socrates returns.*

I surveyed the room. My clothes and all of my worldly possessions were neatly placed in one corner. A chamber pot awaited in the far corner. I adjusted my tunic and ran my fingers through my butchered hair. I pondered my garter which was draped across one of the wooden chairs. Socrates had neither removed it from my waist nor consummated our marriage.

I sat in the other chair and poured myself a quarter cup of wine. I added another quarter cup of water and mixed the drink with my index finger. I licked my finger, gave the mixture another swirl, and then licked my finger again. Had the wine clouded my memory? I checked the bed. No blood.

Am I or am I not a married woman? I mulled this over as I broke off pieces of bread from the basket, softened them in my wine and ate. I did feel strangely different. Hungry and alive. *What is it I de-*

sire? I don't know. But I shouldn't mind being married to a man who treats me as a goddess.

I sprinkled some of the uncut red wine on the bed. *Close enough.* No one but Socrates and I knew the truth. And surely no man would tell such a secret. I admired my handiwork before packing the garter away with my other belongings.

I selected the most aromatic red apple from the basket and was munching contentedly when I heard a light tapping at the door. I wiped the apple's juices from my mouth and considered who it might be. I knew of no one to fear but Xanthippe, who seemed unlikely to tap lightly.

"Come in," I answered.

"Good morning, ma'am," said a young girl. She kept her eyes on the floor and hid behind silky chestnut hair. "Mr. Socrates says to make sure you have whatever you need."

"What is your name, child?" I asked. She reminded me very much of myself when I was eleven and serving my father.

"Korinna, ma'am," she replied shyly.

"Good morning, Korinna." I had indeed been transformed from a "miss" yesterday to a "ma'am" today. "Please have a seat here beside me and tell me about my new home."

Korinna hesitated. Hers was indeed a friendly face. Perhaps she could show me other secret pockets of safety in this home.

"Please join me," I invited her. "I was just enjoying some breakfast."

Korinna glanced back at the open doorway before giving me a slight nod and sitting awkwardly on the very edge of the chair.

"Where is Socrates?" I asked.

"Mr. Socrates and Mr. Lamprocles left for the marketplace at sun-up," she said. "Mr. Socrates always meets his students there."

The sound of scurrying outside the door catapulted Korinna to her feet. An even younger face peeked into the room.

"Iris!" cried Korinna. "What are you doing?"

"I just want to see her, too," the small voice said sheepishly.

"Do come in, child, and let me see you," I coaxed. "Your name is Iris?"

The girl stared at me wide-eyed as she nodded.

"Iris!" Korinna again scolded her. Iris shifted her inquisitive eyes to the basket on the table.

"Are you two sisters?" To their great fortune, neither of them looked anything like Socrates. In fact, I had never heard anyone suggest that Socrates had any daughters.

"Oh, no, ma'am," replied Korinna, "We're not sisters. Mrs. Xanthippe just saved us both."

"Saved you from what, Korinna?"

"Why from exposure, ma'am," Korinna replied.

"And as soon as we're old enough to bring a good price, we'll go live with the richest family she can find," Iris added.

"The nicest family, Iris," Korinna corrected her.

"How many of you has Xanthippe saved?" I pictured the yellow horse trotting up the hillside through the darkness of night drawn by the cries of exposed baby girls. *And why does she save them? Why, to raise them as slaves and sell them for a profit, of course.*

This reality seemed completely lost on Korinna. "There are 14 of us," Korinna told me. "Melissa will be going to her new family soon, so I expect Mrs. Xanthippe'll be looking for another abandoned baby girl to save," Korinna explained. Iris stood close beside her nodding her head.

"Korinna! Iris!" a voice called from the hallway. Both girls froze.

"Yes, Mama Leda," they responded in chorus.

An older woman shuffled through the door and put a hand on each girl's shoulder. The sun had darkened her hands and given her many wrinkles.

"Good morning, Mrs. Myrto," she said in a voice that carried a soothing song through each word. "Did you sleep well?" Her eyes drifted to the bed and stopped briefly on the stained bedding.

I nodded.

"We'll be washing the coverings and anything else you like, ma'am," Mama Leda said, gathering up the blankets from the bed. "Is there anything else you want washed?"

I glanced around the room before shaking my head. *How can I ask you what I really want to know? What am I supposed to do? Where am I supposed to go?*

"Is everything to your liking, ma'am?" Mama Leda asked.

I nodded again and struggled to find the right words. "Mama Leda," I stopped. "Should I call you Mama Leda?"

"You call me whatever you like, ma'am."

I again tried to work out the right questions to get the answers I needed. "What does Socrates call you?" I asked at last.

"Mr. Socrates calls me Leda," she responded. She seemed to sense my true predicament, and shooed Korinna and Iris out the door with the bedding. "You girls go on. Get started on the wash now."

Once they were safely out of earshot, Leda turned her attention back to me. "Mr. Socrates told me to show you around the place, answer all of your questions, and make sure you have everything you need until he returns."

I walked around the room, running my hands along the chairs and table. "When will he be back?" I asked.

"That's hard to say, ma'am. Usually by sunset, but sometimes not until closer to sunrise." She paused to see if I had another question. After several moments, she broke the silence. "Let me introduce you to Zoe the cook. Then we'll see if we can find Praxis. He does most of the farming and the buying and selling at the market."

And so I allowed Leda to extract me from the safety of Socrates' chambers and lead me into the fearsome house of Xanthippe.

6

LEDA WALKED ME through the common rooms of the house and into the courtyard where Xanthippe lay in wait. Again I heard her before I saw her.

"So, this is the soil of Aristides the Just where Socrates wants to plant his seed!" Xanthippe roared. I spun to face her. Her dark brown eyes pierced mine with a jolting force. My body wrenched backward. I steadied myself and fixed my eyes upon her leather sandals.

Leda stepped between us. "Yes, ma'am," she mumbled.

"Well, forgive me for not celebrating when the old goat tracks dirt into my house." Xanthippe spat on the ground in my direction. My face flushed and my ears burned as Xanthippe continued her tirade.

"Socrates can keep all the filth he likes in his own bed chambers. I'll never set foot in there again; but you, Miss Myrto, will do well to get it into that pretty little head of yours that this is my house, and you best not set foot in it unless you intend to do exactly as I say!"

Anger seized my chest, and tears began to sting my eyes. Before a sound could pass through my quivering lips, I retreated to Socrates' room and hurled myself on the bed. Arms wrapped around my stomach, I shook violently from head to toe. "Oh, Athena, goddess of war and wisdom, what am I to do?" I cried in quiet whispers. "Surely I cannot win a war against Xanthippe!"

My mind returned to my garter. *I should have ended this before it ever began. Perhaps it's not too late.* I sat up and dried my eyes. The wine on the table called to me, and I answered, hands trembling as I poured the first cup. *Would I be better off dead? Is there any hope for me?*

I drank the strong wine quickly before leaning back in a chair to catch my breath. I was well into my second cup when Leda returned to check on me.

"Are you all right?" she asked. Her arms were full of fresh bedding, and she set to work making the bed without waiting for a response.

"Leda, what am I going to do?" I wailed. "How can I possibly stay here?"

"She does have quite the temper, ma'am; there's no denying it." Leda let out a burst of air that sounded like a soft chuckle, followed by a cough to disguise it. I felt betrayed by her amusement.

"I've known Mrs. Xanthippe her whole life, and you can believe me when I tell you that I think you've survived the worst of it." Leda finished making up the bed and walked over toward the chamber pot. "She's always got a mean bark, but she hardly ever attacks."

"But you heard what she said," I argued. "I never should have set foot in this house."

"Mrs. Myrto, this all came up very sudden-like for Mrs. Xanthippe." Leda said. "Why it was only the night before last that Mr. Socrates announced most unexpectedly that he would be taking a second wife."

I tried to imagine that conversation. Had the Socrates that promised to treat me as a goddess somehow tamed the yellow horse? My heart and head were still pounding. I went back to the bed to lie down.

"As the gods are my witness, they had the most fiery argument I've heard in years," Leda confided. "The young girls were cowering in their beds, and Mr. Lamprocles left the house altogether."

"Do tell me what they said," I beseeched her.

"Oh, they moved from room to room, and I don't pretend to have listened in on every word, but I can tell you that they ended up in this very room."

I pushed the image of Xanthippe and Socrates together in this room out of my mind. "She said she'd never set foot in this room again," I reminded Leda.

"Oh, she told Mr. Socrates that, too," Leda said. I scooted my body up in the bed and propped myself up on my elbows. I stared hard at Leda who was trying to hide a smile, but couldn't keep her belly from shaking with laughter. "Right after she dumped this here chamber pot on top of Mr. Socrates' head, she swore by the graves of her parents that she would never set foot in this room again."

"No!" I was aghast at the very thought. "Surely not the chamber pot!" I whistled under my breath in disbelief. *How could any woman in the world have such daring?* "What did Socrates do?" I asked.

"He chuckled and said that rain almost always follows the thunder," Leda responded. "And then he proceeded to clean up the mess. With my help, of course."

Part of me hated Xanthippe more than I'd ever hated anyone or anything in my life, but somewhere inside me a kernel of admiration took root. I tried to ask myself what I would do if I were her, but I had no experience at being a woman or being married or bearing and raising a man's children. All I knew is that I had never stood up to any man, or even another woman. *I would have swallowed my anger and let it devour me from within.*

"So what should I do, Leda?" I asked in earnest.

"I cannot rightly say, ma'am," Leda responded, shaking her head. Slaves were not normally called upon to tell their owners what to do.

"But you know both Xanthippe and Socrates," I pleaded. "What would you do if you were me? Xanthippe surely hates me."

Leda seemed to ponder the question. "She has no reason to like you, it's true. Just don't give her any real cause to hate you. It won't be long before she finds something entirely different to thunder about."

"And until then?" I asked. "Am I to stay hidden away in this room all day?"

"Mr. Socrates would be the one to talk to about that, ma'am," Leda replied. "I just came in to make the bed and empty the chamber pot. Is there anything else I can get you for now?"

I let my body fall back onto the bed. "No. Thank you, Leda. I'll be fine." I closed my eyes and breathed deeply. The wine was relaxing me and telling me that perhaps I really would be all right. Socrates would come home and talk to me of desires. Until he returned I would deliberate more on this question. *What is it that I desire?*

7

MY FIRST DAY of marriage was the first day of my life I had nothing to do—no cooking, no cleaning, no weaving, no planting, no tending to the animals, no caring for Father. Nothing. I asked myself a hundred times what I should do. What could I do? I paced about the room, imploring the gods for a sign.

Then suddenly it occurred to me. *I am married to the wisest man in the world. I will ask Socrates, and he will tell me what I am to do. I will do what my husband tells me to do. This will surely please the gods and Socrates.* This resolution brought great relief. I lay down on the bed and offered myself up to sleep. My dreams carried me out of Socrates' room, away from Xanthippe's house, back to my own bed where I slept soundly.

When I awoke, the lamp on the table at the foot of Socrates' bed shone brightly upon a plate of ripe olives, goat cheese and barley bread. Beside the food were two jars, one of water and one of wine. I poured myself a cup of water. *I am not welcome at Xanthippe's table. Am I to eat alone from now on?* I studied the food before me. It certainly looked delicious. Probably the finest in the house. *Who brought me this beautiful meal? Certainly not Xanthippe.*

At the thought of Xanthippe, fear completely replaced my loneliness. Perhaps Xanthippe had prepared my supper—an enticing presentation laced with poison. *Are my suspicions merely wishful thinking? What do I desire?* Nothing. I stared at the plate, lost in my indifference.

I was still staring at the plate when Socrates returned.

"Good evening, Myrto," he said with a smile. "May I join you?"

I nodded. Socrates pulled the other chair up beside me and poured himself a glass of wine.

"Aren't you hungry?" he asked.

I shook my head.

Socrates frowned. "Is there something you need?"

I nodded and took a deep breath to summon my courage. "I have food and drink and a place to rest. But I have nothing to do. What would you have me do?"

Socrates shrugged. "Do what you like." He tipped his wine glass toward me before taking a drink.

"Socrates, you are my husband. You are the wisest of all men. I would like for you to tell me what I should do." I drank from my cup, wishing it were wine rather than water.

"I am your husband, this is true. But why do you call me wise?"

I drank the rest of my water and thought about the stories I'd heard. "Everyone says that the priestess of Apollo in Delphi told Chaerophon that you are the wisest of all men. The Delphic Oracle cannot lie."

Socrates laughed and poured himself some more wine. I slid my glass toward him, and he filled it as well. "Just because the Oracle cannot lie, does not mean those who hear the truth will understand it."

"You speak in riddles," I said, shaking my head. "I don't understand."

"Have you heard of Croesus, the mighty king of Lydia who consulted the Oracle because he wished to wage war on Persia?" Socrates took a piece of bread and some cheese.

I nodded. "Everyone knows this history."

"And what did the priestess tell him?"

"That Croesus would destroy a great kingdom," I replied.

"Exactly," said Socrates. "So what did Croesus do?"

"He attacked Persia," I said.

"And did he destroy the great kingdom of Persia?" Socrates asked.

"No," I replied. "The great kingdom he destroyed was his own."

Socrates nodded. "Have some food and I will tell you exactly what Chaerophon told me." Socrates pushed the plate toward me.

I drank most of my wine before taking a handful of olives and placing them in my mouth one at a time. The flesh fell easily away from each pit as I bit down. I collected the pits between my cheek and gum, sucking the salty brine completely from every one.

"Chaerophon was my friend from youth," Socrates began. "He always was so impulsive. I have no idea what possessed him to travel to Delphi and waste an audience with the priestess to inquire about my supposed wisdom."

I put my hand to my mouth, curling my fingers around my lips and sliding the pits out of my mouth into my cupped hand. When my mouth was clear, I asked, "You did not send him?"

Socrates leaned back in his chair and laughed. "My dear, I have always known that I am not wise. I had no idea he was going. It was only after he returned and began spreading slander about my supposed wisdom that I asked him to tell me exactly what he had asked the Oracle." Socrates paused for another bite of cheese and bread.

"So what was Chaerophon's question?" I asked.

"Chaerophon intended to ask if I possessed true wisdom, but as he approached the great temple of Apollo, excitement overtook him."

"I've heard that the Oracle in Delphi is as big as the Parthenon here in Athens," I said, trying to imagine how terrifying it would be to stand so close to a god and live to tell about it.

Socrates nodded. "Chaerophon said he read the three great inscriptions as he passed through the gates: 'Know Thyself,' 'All Things in Moderation,' and 'Promises Lead to Perdition.' He felt open to hearing and understanding the truth. But then when he entered the cell of the god, it was so narrow that the walls pressed in upon him." Socrates filled both of our cups with wine before he continued.

"Inside the great temple of Apollo, behind the confining cell, the priestess stood in a small underground crypt filled with smoke. She was chewing laurel leaves and speaking in a terrifying frenzy to the man in line before him. Chaerophon trembled with the most tremendous fear. He was still quite overwhelmed when they summoned him for his audience. So when it was his turn, he did not ask if I possessed true wisdom. Instead, he asked, 'Is any man wiser than Socrates?'"

"And what did the priestess say?" I asked.

"Of course, Chaerophon could not understand a word she said. But the priests interpreted her utterances to say, 'No one is wiser.'"

"So you *are* the wisest man of all!" I exclaimed.

Socrates shook his head. "That's what Chaerophon thought, too, but that's not what the Oracle said. The Oracle did not say that I was wise, only that no one was wiser."

"Isn't that the same thing?" I asked.

"For a long time I pondered this," Socrates replied. "I've spent years investigating the wisdom of everyone with a reputation for being wise. I examine each man and especially those who believe themselves to be wise. And do you know what I've found?"

I shook my head.

"That not one of these men can explain anything worthwhile. I've talked to politicians and poets, philosophers and teachers. The more they try to explain what they know, the more obvious it becomes that they do not really know. There are so many questions they cannot answer about what they profess to know. Yet each remains adamant about his own knowledge. They all think they know something when they do not."

"Isn't there anyone who is wise?" I asked.

Socrates shook his head. "All of the human wisdom I've found has been worth little or nothing. If I am wise in any way, it's only because I at least understand that I know nothing."

"So what about all of the men you questioned who were supposed to be wise?"

"Well," Socrates said with a sad smile, "they still call themselves wise." Then his eyes sparkled as he looked into mine. "And they aren't very fond of me." He held my gaze for a moment before I looked away.

We continued eating in silence. Finally, I decided to ask him again. "Even if you are not wise, you are still my husband. What is it that you would have me do each day?"

"Do what you like," Socrates replied.

"How can I do what I like?" I asked. "I am a prisoner in this room, afraid to set foot in Xanthippe's house and with nowhere else to go outside this house."

Socrates took my hand in his. "You are not a prisoner in this house, Myrto. You are free to come and go as you please. Where do you want to go? What do you want to spend your days doing?"

Tears filled my eyes and rolled down my cheeks.

"There is nowhere," I said, shaking my head. "There is nothing."

Socrates brought my hand to his lips. "There is everywhere and everything. If you wish, tomorrow you may come with me."

8

SOCRATES AWAKENED ME before dawn. "Myrto," he said gently shaking me. "Do you wish to join me today?"

I sat up and rubbed the dreams from my eyes. "I do," I said, my words swallowed up in a yawn. I stretched my arms and yawned again.

Socrates captured my hand in his and pulled me gently toward him. The warmth of his breath sent a pleasant tremble through my body as he kissed my forehead. "Please dress and meet me in the courtyard," Socrates said. He smiled, released my hand, and left the room.

Lamprocles and Socrates were both waiting when I entered the enclosed patio. Bird songs filled the chilly morning air. Mountain crickets hummed and distant pond frogs crooned their accompaniment. A gentle breeze beckoned me to step into the unknown.

Lamprocles broke the spell with an awkward greeting. "Morning, Myrto." He was holding a torch in one hand and a satchel in the other. The torch illuminated his wavy hair and the fuzzy wisps of his first whiskers.

I nodded and murmured a polite response. Socrates wrapped a cloak around my shoulders and turned me toward the gate. "Shall we?" he said, motioning to Lamprocles to lead the way.

I could hardly believe it. I was going to spend the day in the Agora and taste the daily activity of Athens' marketplace. *Respectable women know only the flurry of festival days. What husband has ever invited his wife to share the wonder of an average day? Is it even allowed?* Socrates strolled along between Lamprocles and me as if I were just another son.

"Is there anything that you would like to discuss as we walk?" Socrates asked, looking first to me and then to Lamprocles. I shook my head and leaned back to catch a glimpse of Lamprocles.

"No, Father," Lamprocles replied.

"Very well," Socrates said. "Then let us think about wisdom. Does either of you know what wisdom is?"

Lamprocles shuffled his feet in the dusty road, turning up a large stone. He kicked it in the opposite direction, but somehow I felt as if it were directed at me.

"Myrto," said Socrates, "what is wisdom?"

I wanted desperately to give the right answer so that Lamprocles would think well of me and Socrates would be proud of me. *What could it possibly be? Did Socrates give me a clue last night?*

"Last night you told me that you are not wise," I ventured. "So I suppose wisdom must be something that you do not possess."

Socrates laughed aloud. "Excellent start, my dear! Don't you agree, Lamprocles?" Socrates' left hand caught my right hand, raising it to his lips. His kiss of approval ran up my arm and moved my own lips to smile.

"It's a start, but I cannot agree that you do not possess wisdom, Father," replied Lamprocles. "Your wisdom is your understanding that you know nothing."

"Ah, I see," said Socrates, gently releasing my hand. "So wisdom is a kind of understanding?"

"Yes," said Lamprocles. "It must be so."

Socrates again turned to me. "Would you agree, Myrto?"

"I would agree that I am not wise," I said, "because I do not understand. You say you are not wise, but Lamprocles and your students believe you are wise and hope to learn wisdom from you." Somewhere ahead the sound of squeals and scurrying hooves brought to life my own feelings of confusion.

"She's got a point, my boy," said Socrates. "Perhaps we must first discuss whether wisdom is a kind of knowledge that can be taught."

Lamprocles grumbled something under his breath and found another stone to kick as we walked along the path. I looked past him to the deep purple saturating the eastern sky with hope for a new day.

"And if it can be taught, who is wise enough to teach it?" continued Socrates.

"Only the gods are truly wise," Lamprocles replied.

Socrates turned back to me. "What do you think, Myrto?"

The questions swirled in my brain. *What do I think? What an odd idea. I can think. Do my thoughts even matter?* The road crested atop the small hill allowing us to see a scruffy drover with his herd of grunting pigs on their way to the market before us.

"I agree with Lamprocles," I said.

"Agreement does not require thought," retorted Lamprocles. "Father asked you what you think. You can't just agree."

The harshness of these words pricked my heart. I walked on, silenced by the shame of my confusion. Socrates combed his fingers through his beard, but did not say a word. They both waited for my reply.

"I don't know," I said finally.

"Then you must think about what it is you do not know and ask a question aimed to find out," replied Lamprocles.

There is so much I do not know. How can I think about all of it? I pondered this as I watched the road ahead. Though the sky was still mostly dark, I could see the swine overtaking a long-bearded farmer carrying a cage of chickens in each hand. The drover's dog barked and circled to herd the pigs, but it was heading them right into the farmer who was shouting unimaginable curses.

I, too, felt like cursing. *Sacred Athena! I don't know! And my husband won't tell me! Instead, he claims to know nothing!* Gradually a question formed in my mind. "Socrates says he knows nothing, but isn't that something?" I looked from Socrates' serene smile to Lamprocles' furrowed brow.

Lamprocles stared at Socrates, who again remained silent. "It may be something, but it is not wisdom. I think it is experience. Don't you have experience, Father? More experience than Myrto and I combined!"

"I've certainly lived longer," conceded Socrates. "I have been a sculptor and a soldier, a husband and a father. These experiences are different than yours, but I can't say that they are more."

"But you can share your experiences with us and we can learn from them, right?" asked Lamprocles.

"That's an interesting thought," said Socrates, and Lamprocles looked pleased. "I wonder if one can truly learn from another's experience."

"Isn't that the basis of all apprenticeships?" Lamprocles asked. "A young man learns his trade from an experienced blacksmith or cobbler or ship maker."

"It seems to me that the young apprentice learns from his own observation of the master and his own experience working with the master," Socrates countered. "Who would you hold accountable for what the apprentice learns?

"Why, the master, of course," replied Lamprocles.

"Can the master somehow transfer his experience to the apprentice?" asked Socrates.

"No, of course not," replied Lamprocles. "The young apprentice must gain his own experience."

"So then the young apprentice is responsible for his own experience, what he chooses to study and think and learn for himself?" asked Socrates.

"Yes," agreed Lamprocles.

Socrates reached out for my hand and pulled me back into the conversation. "Myrto, do you think the same is true of teachers and students?"

"I would suppose so," I replied.

"Is there a question that you can ask that would help you discover what you think?" Socrates prodded.

I shrugged.

"Teachers teach, right?" said Lamprocles.

I nodded.

"What do students do?" asked Lamprocles.

"Students learn?" I offered timidly.

"And which is more important?" Lamprocles probed further. "Which is the objective—teaching or learning?"

"Learning," I said, this time with more conviction.

"And who does the learning?" Lamprocles asked.

"Students," I replied.

"Precisely!" exclaimed Socrates. "This is why I have never claimed to be a teacher or charged fathers for the time I spend with their sons. I cannot teach anyone anything. I can only help him,"

Socrates paused and looked me directly in the eyes, "or *her*, to learn."

We entered Athens at the break of dawn. As we passed through the city gate, the noisy business of living surrounded us. Donkey carts overflowing with produce impeded foot traffic on the narrow streets. Gentlemen dressed in their best white mantels pressed onward, careful to avoid the mud and manure. A group of soldiers talked brusquely and laughed loudly, shields and spears clattering.

Our conversation succumbed to the raucous crowd. In the midst of the noise, I felt a strange quiet within me. Each breath brought a different sweet or pungent odor of city life. My body absorbed the chaotic energy and surged with excitement. Regardless of what lay ahead, at that moment, for the first time in my life, I desired to be exactly where I was.

9

WE FLOWED WITH the stream of people from the constricted roadways into the openness of the Agora. A sea of men flooded the marketplace. I stayed close to Socrates and searched the multitudes for other women. Aside from the girls selling flowers and several women selling bread, there were none.

We walked past the fish vendors and away from the crowd. Beneath a bay tree, a small group of men sat chatting. They shouted greetings as we approached.

"Good morning, Socrates!" said one, jumping to his feet and rushing to meet us. The breadth of his forehead matched the breadth of his shoulders. He nodded toward Lamprocles, then turned to me with a look of wonder. Lamprocles returned the nod and went on to greet the others.

"Allow me to introduce you to Myrto, daughter of Lysimachus," said Socrates.

"Granddaughter of Aristides the Just?" the man inquired.

"The very same." Socrates nodded. "Myrto, may I present Aristocles, son of Ariston."

Aristocles took my right hand in both his hands and held it. "You can call me Plato." He smiled. "All my friends do." His arms were strong like a soldier, but his hands were soft and well-oiled. I guessed him to be about 25 years old and wondered if he was married. His loose curls rested on his shoulders, but his tawny beard was neatly trimmed.

"Good morning," I said. I slipped my hand away from between his. Socrates had already moved on toward the others. I quickened my pace to catch up to my husband. Plato matched my stride.

"Are you a student of Aspasia?" he asked, slowing to nearly a stop. His question held me back with him.

Me? A student? I shook my head. Aspasia of Miletus was the mistress of the great ruler Pericles. Pericles died of the plague before I was born, but I had heard that Aspasia still educated young women in music and the arts.

"I just thought that since Socrates was once a student of Aspasia and now here you are with Socrates . . . well, I thought maybe she sent you to study with Socrates."

I stopped. "Socrates was a student of Aspasia?" I asked. I looked over at the old man surrounded by youth beneath the speckled sun and shade of the bay leaves. *Is there nothing ordinary about him?*

"Why do you seem so surprised?" asked Plato. "Socrates is always saying that Connus taught him to play music and Aspasia taught him the art of public speaking."

I shrugged my shoulders. Part of me felt I should join Socrates immediately, but part of me wanted to hear more of what Plato might say.

The rising sun shone brightly upon us. Plato turned me gently so that we were facing each other without the sun in our eyes. "Do you like poetry?" Plato asked.

I nodded.

"I absolutely adore the poetry of Sappho," said Plato. "Only the nine muses can compare." He stood straight and breathed in deeply, as if to command the attention of the gods. "On your dappled throne, Aphrodite, cunning daughter of Zeus. I beg you, do not crush my heart with pain, oh lady."

A strange rushing swept my chest and warmth gathered in my cheeks. I stepped to one side to look past Plato and look again at my husband. Plato was much more like the man I had always pictured myself marrying.

"Forgive me, Myrto," said Plato. "You've inspired me with your beauty, and I've offended you by being so forward."

I shook my head. I meant to clear my impious thoughts more than to disagree.

"I also have many poems of Solon," Plato offered. "My family traces its roots back to him directly. I've got the most complete collection of his writings that you'll find anywhere in the world. If you like, I'll let you borrow some. You may read them at your leisure."

I turned back to Plato, who was looking at me curiously. *He thinks I can read.* "You're very kind," I said.

"And you're very perplexing," Plato replied. "What brings you to the Agora with Socrates and Lamprocles?"

"Socrates invited me to come," I said.

"He did?" Plato glanced over at Socrates. "Those who are loathe to have him teach young men will be absolutely scandalized to think he may begin corrupting young women as well!" His eyes returned to me. "I, however, rather like the idea of inviting beautiful young women to join our discussions."

"I am not here to be corrupted!" I said more assertively than I'd ever spoken to anyone, women and slaves included, but the fact remained that custom required me to be in the home, not in the marketplace among men. *But it's my husband who suggested I come.* Surely there was nothing immoral about a woman accepting her husband's invitation to join him in the Agora.

"I feel as if I'm missing something," said Plato, shaking his head. He looked at my waist. Out in public for the first time without my garter belt, I suddenly felt exposed. "Are you married?" Plato asked.

I nodded.

"And your husband? Where is he?"

I gestured toward the tree.

"Young Lamprocles? You must be joking!" Plato exclaimed.

I shook my head. "Not Lamprocles. Socrates."

"Now I'm sure you're playing with me," laughed Plato.

I shook my head again. "Socrates is my husband."

Plato laughed harder. "Oh, yes! You're exactly the little woman that Xanthippe would choose to bear more sons for her husband!"

A ball of anger and confusion rose in my throat. I struggled to spit it out. "I can assure you Xanthippe is not pleased." I wanted to run home. My home. All the way back to my childhood before Mother died. Back to a world that was safe and made sense. *There is no place for me to run.* I straightened my back with determination and walked toward my husband. I could feel Plato watching my back, but he did not follow me.

The men were in the midst of a rather heated discussion. Lamprocles glared at me. *Oh, yes, it could be worse. I may not be married to someone as desirable as Plato, but at least I'm not married to Lamprocles!* Without meaning to, I smiled. Lamprocles scowled. The only one who seemed to be completely at ease was Socrates. He gestured for me to have a seat by his side.

"Gentlemen, this is Myrto," said Socrates. "She'll be joining me for as long as she chooses."

The men nodded their greetings, but continued arguing. Everyone was talking at once.

"I don't trust him, I tell you. He's too close to the Thirty Tyrants!"

"It's true. Charmides is his uncle and Critias himself is a cousin."

"They've ordered the execution of Alcibiades!"

"Socrates could be next!"

Socrates winked at me and cleared his throat. Every head turned to hear him speak. "Do you mind if I summarize our discussion for Myrto?

"Please do, Socrates," the men all agreed.

"Very well," Socrates began. He pointed to two men on his left as he spoke. "Ever since Sparta defeated Athens and imposed the reign of the Thirty Tyrants, Dion and Megellus here have been plotting to overthrow the Tyrants and restore democracy to our people." The two men nodded their agreement.

"The Tyrants destroyed our city when they tore down the long walls that protected us and connected us to the sea," said Megellus.

"And Critias himself celebrated during the ruin by dancing and playing his flute," added Dion.

"Of course, he was celebrating," said Lamprocles. "He's the leader of the whole, rotten bunch!"

"Critias and Charmides," growled Dion. "Two peas in a pod!"

"And your friend Plato hails from the same vine," chimed in Lamprocles. He was looking directly at me. At least ten years younger than all of the other men here, Lamprocles seemed a bit out of place, too. He and I were the only ones without beards.

"Their days are numbered," said a man to our right.

"You speak the truth, Theages!" proclaimed a chorus of voices.

"What do you say, Socrates?" asked Dion.

"I say we must continue to examine the path to justice," said Socrates. "Have decades of war brought us justice?"

"No," the men agreed.

"Have politicians and tyrants brought us justice?"

"No," sang the chorus again.

"Then we who love Athens and love wisdom, must ask ourselves, what is the justice we seek," Socrates said.

"But what about Plato?" asked Megellus. "Can we trust him?"

"When we were at war, did Plato take up his sword and fight?" asked Socrates.

"He did," replied Dion. "He fought bravely for Athens for at least four years."

"Is there anyone who loves wisdom and justice more than Plato?" asked Socrates.

"Only you, Socrates," said Theages.

"If that is true," said Socrates, "it is only because I have loved them longer."

Socrates admiration for Plato seemed most genuine. Perhaps if I became a lover of wisdom and justice, I, too, would earn my husband's approval.

10

THE DAY PASSED quickly with conversations here and there throughout the marketplace. Food and drink appeared with no apparent exchange of money. I quietly and gratefully soaked it all in, still wondering how one becomes a lover of wisdom.

Thoughts and questions swirled in my mind as we walked home from the Agora. Unlike the morning journey, few traveled the road outside the city wall. Lamprocles alone spoke. His voice buzzed on in my ear about Plato and the Thirty Tyrants and Alcibiades. *What does any of this have to do with me as a woman?*

"Alcibiades calls himself your student!" exclaimed Lamprocles. "People will say he learned his treachery from you. Plato calls himself your student, too!" Lamprocles continued. "What will people think?"

Socrates strolled along at a leisurely pace. "People will think what they want to think." He looked at me and smiled. "They always do, you know."

Lamprocles huffed and shook his head. "But you're turning everyone against you. And for what? It's not like they've paid you anything."

Socrates shrugged. "I'm only interested in discovering Truth and Goodness. You can't buy that with money."

"The truth is that the Thirty Tyrants want to kill you," retorted Lamprocles. "And if they don't get the chance, the citizens of Athens will do it for them if they think you're in cahoots with Alcibiades."

I waited for Socrates to dispute these accusations. He did not. Nor did he look the least bit concerned. *Can someone seeking Goodness acquire mortal enemies?*

"Is what Lamprocles says true?" I finally asked. Still, my concern was my own. Socrates' death would leave me in an even worse place than my father's had. My brother Aristides might have no choice but to give me to Uncle or sell me into slavery.

Socrates raised his eyebrows and shrugged his shoulders.

"Of course it's true!" cried Lamprocles. "Last week the Thirty summoned Father and four others to the hall and ordered them to bring Leon from Salamis to be executed. And do you know what Father did?"

I stared at Socrates who appeared as serene as ever. "No, I don't," I replied.

"Tell her, Father," insisted Lamprocles. "Tell your new wife of the danger you're in."

A coldness overcame me. I pulled my cloak more tightly around my shoulders and waited to hear what Socrates would say.

Socrates cleared his throat. "I did what any just and pious person would do," he replied.

"The other four men ran to Salamis to get Leon," said Lamprocles. "They brought him directly to the Tyrants for execution."

"Leon did nothing to deserve execution. His blood is on their hands, not mine," said Socrates.

"No one seems to mind having Leon's blood on their hands," said Lamprocles. "And now that you've directly disobeyed the Thirty Tyrants, they'll mind your blood on their hands even less!"

Socrates said nothing.

"Is he really in danger?" I asked Lamprocles. I tried to keep Socrates' calm, easy pace, but inside I was running with Lamprocles.

"What do you think?" Lamprocles snapped. "How long do you think the Tyrants will let someone live who directly defies them?"

Lamprocles turned to me. "And don't think people didn't notice that he's teaching young women now, too." He looked to Socrates. "If they disapprove of your influence over the young men of Athens, what will they say about including young women among your followers?"

"She is my wife," Socrates said sternly. "I may do with her as I please."

Tears welled up in my eyes. Impiety of any sort could be charged as a crime punishable by death. *If something happens to Socrates, where will I go? What will become of me?*

Socrates' face softened as he looked upon me once again. "It's not as bad as all that," he said, taking my hand. "I fought face to face against Spartans, swords in hand and raised to kill me. During the campaigns in Amphipolis, Delium and Potidaea—I was in real danger then." Socrates lifted my hand to his lips. "Yet here I am, alive and well, right here with you."

My heartbeat quickened. Warmth returned to my body.

"Potidaea!" Lamprocles spat on the ground. "I curse that Corinthian colony where you saved Alcibiades. The traitor!"

52

"Ah, Lamprocles," Socrates laughed. "Alcibiades did repay me by rescuing me from certain death in Delium." His laughter was not unkind.

"He's still a traitor to Athens!" Lamprocles insisted.

Socrates shook his head. "Alcibiades is as brilliant as he is beautiful. Men and women alike have worshipped him and felt betrayed."

"Alcibiades loves no one but himself," said Lamprocles. "He betrays all who love him without remorse."

"And that is precisely why he stands accused by both Spartans and Athenians," Socrates conceded. "Perhaps he is a traitor or perhaps he is merely human like the rest of us, doubly cursed by talent and beauty."

My emotions tossed to and fro between Lamprocles' anger and Socrates' tranquility. I wanted to believe Socrates, but I feared Lamprocles was right. If not about me, at least about Alcibiades. I pushed thoughts of Plato from my mind. *So many thoughts. So many feelings. The floodgates have opened. Rushing waters carry me downstream. I gasp for breath.*

I must have gasped aloud. Socrates and Lamprocles both stopped. They looked at me.

"Are you all right?" asked Socrates.

I nodded.

Socrates took both of my hands in his. "What are you thinking?" His full attention filled me with courage.

"You both say different things, but you both sound like you're telling the truth. How can that be?"

Socrates put an arm around my waist and a hand on Lamprocles shoulder. The three of us walked on. Socrates was not ignoring my question. Instead, the three of us pondered it as we walked.

Socrates spoke first. "I am a man," he said. He paused as if this were somehow the answer to my question. "Is that a true statement?"

"Yes," I replied. Lamprocles voice echoed mine.

"Are you both quite certain?" Socrates persisted.

"Yes," Lamprocles and I answered in unison, our voices filled with confidence.

"Very well," replied Socrates. He turned to me. "Now you say it. Make the same statement I just made."

"I am a man," I offered. I suddenly felt foolish and ashamed.

"Now, Lamprocles," said Socrates. "Is that a true statement?"

Lamprocles sighed. "No. That is not a true statement."

Socrates nodded. "Now you repeat the statement, Lamprocles."

Lamprocles inhaled deeply. "I am a man!" he proclaimed.

Socrates turned to me. "Is this statement true?"

I looked at Lamprocles. He clenched his jaw and awaited my judgment. I took a deep breath. "If it is not, it most certainly will be soon," I replied gently.

Socrates nodded, and Lamprocles gave me his first smile.

"Myrto," said Socrates. "Even when I do my best to tell you and Lamprocles the truth, you cannot simply repeat what I say as truth for yourself. If you wish to tell the truth, you each must speak your own words from your own experience."

We walked on in a comfortable silence. As we neared the house, Lamprocles asked, "What is black with three heads and two arms and doomed to die at sunset?"

"An excellent riddle, my boy!" said Socrates, sliding his hand off Lamprocles' shoulder and patting him on the back.

I imagined a monster with the heads of three black panthers and the arms of Achilles, sword in hand, poised to kill or be killed.

"What do you think, Myrto?" asked Socrates.

"I cannot imagine," I replied.

"Nor can I," agreed Socrates, "but it reminds me of the Sphinx's riddle that only Oedipus could solve. Do you know that riddle?"

I nodded. Everyone knew the story of Oedipus the King. "What walks on four legs in the morning, two legs at noon, and three legs in the evening?" I said.

"Exactly," said Lamprocles. "And the answer to that riddle can be a clue to my riddle."

"The answer to the Sphinx's riddle was man," I said, "because he crawls as a child, walks upright as an adult and requires a cane in his old age."

"Does that give you a clue to Lamprocles' riddle?" asked Socrates. His eyes twinkled with delight.

I pictured the Sphinx with three heads and a pair of arms hanging out of one mouth as she devoured the poor souls who failed to solve her riddle. I shook my head. "I'm afraid I still don't know," I confessed.

Socrates turned to Lamprocles. "Do tell us. What is black with three heads and two arms and doomed to die at sunset?"

Lamprocles grinned. "The shadow of an old man, a young man and a young woman," he said pointing east, to the long shadow traveling beside us.

Tears of happiness and sadness combined and rolled down my cheeks. This was the best day ever, coming to a close.

Bright red and orange banners streaked the evening sky welcoming us home. Leda, Korinna and Iris greeted us and washed the dust from our feet. A table set for three offered cheese and bread, olives and fruit for dinner.

"Where is Mother?" Lamprocles asked Leda.

"She and Praxis took Melissa to her new home," said Leda. "I don't expect them back for a while yet."

Thank you, Athena. I ate hungrily and crawled off to bed. A deep, dreamless sleep overcame me the instant I rested my head on the pillow.

11

THE FAST, RATTLING song of a warbler awakened me before dawn. Socrates lay beside me in the bed. I rolled over on my side and moved closer to him. His body radiated heat in the cool darkness of morning. He turned over to face me. I had never lain so close to a man, yet I did not feel afraid.

He reached out and gently stroked my cheek. "Good morning, Myrto," he whispered.

I captured his hand with mine, kissed it, and pressed it against my cheek. "Yesterday in the Agora I discovered my first desire," I confided.

Socrates nodded. "And what is it?" he asked.

"I want to learn to read," I replied.

Socrates rolled to his back and held my hand to his chest. "Then you shall," he said. "You shall begin today."

We dressed and readied ourselves for the day. We found Lamprocles already in the courtyard eating wine-soaked bread. He motioned for us to have some.

"Good morning, Lamprocles," said Socrates. He scooped a large chunk of bread from the plate to his mouth. "I have a favor to ask of you."

"What is it, Father?" asked Lamprocles.

"You will need your wooden tablet," Socrates replied. "Do you know where it is?"

"Yes. Shall I get it now?" asked Lamprocles.

Socrates nodded. As Lamprocles left, Socrates pulled out a scroll and opened it before me. "What do you see, Myrto?" Socrates asked.

"I see a book," I said.

"Look more closely at the writing," said Socrates. "What do you see?"

"Nothing but lines and squiggly marks," I confessed.

Socrates nodded. "The next time you look at this book, your eyes will see words that speak silently to your mind, yet deeply affect your thoughts."

Excitement and anticipation churned within me, giving new life to my desire.

Lamprocles returned with the tablet. "I smoothed the wax," Lamprocles said eagerly. He held a small pointed stick poised to write. "I am ready to write whatever you say, Father."

"Write the alphabet, please," Socrates requested.

Lamprocles looked puzzled. "Just the alphabet?"

"Yes, from alpha to omega, every letter," said Socrates.

Lamprocles began writing. I watched, imagining myself sitting there swiftly marking down each letter of the alphabet.

When Lamprocles finished, Socrates asked, "Could you teach an intelligent person the entire alphabet in a single day?"

Lamprocles studied the tablet. "I could teach him to recognize each letter and the sound it represents," replied Lamprocles. "It would take a little longer for him to be able to write each letter well himself."

"Not himself," said Socrates. "Herself." He motioned toward me.

"Today while we are all in the Agora, I would like for you to teach Myrto the letters of the alphabet," said Socrates.

I held my breath as Lamprocles looked from the tablet to me and back to the tablet. "I can do that," he said finally, "on one condition."

Socrates smiled. "And what might that be?"

Lamprocles handed me the tablet and stick, then crossed his arms sternly. "Myrto must agree to learn, and to work even harder at learning than I do at teaching."

"Oh, I will!" I exclaimed. "I promise I will. I am grateful to have you as my teacher."

"Very well then," said Socrates. "It's settled. We can discuss the name and sound of each letter as we walk. Let us begin so that we can be in the marketplace by sunrise."

We arrived at the Agora in no time. I marveled that all of the words we speak consist of only 24 basic sounds. And by our journey home that evening, I knew them all. Of course, it helped that the letters were the same words we used for counting and that the sounds seemed to come from the words themselves. Lamprocles agreed to continue teaching me, not just sounds and letters, but truly to read and write.

Socrates and Lamprocles had dinner with Xanthippe, but I took my plate to the bedroom and spent the rest of the evening with the tablet, carefully forming each letter of the alphabet I'd learned in the wax, repeating each sound as I wrote. I wrote until my hand throbbed and I could hardly grasp the writing stick in my fingers.

As we walked to the Agora the following day, Lamprocles and Socrates discussed my reading curriculum.

"You can practice names, words and sentences with the tablet this morning," said Socrates. "By afternoon, I'll find you an actual text to begin reading."

"Shall we start with Homer's *Iliad?*" asked Lamprocles. "That's where my school teachers started when I was a young boy."

"Your teachers started with *The Iliad* and *The Odyssey* because they were stories most boys had already learned by heart," said Socrates.

"It's true," agreed Lamprocles. "We were only half reading and half reciting."

"Every young boy loves the stories of the mighty warrior Achilles and the crafty adventurer Odysseus," said Socrates. "But I wonder if that is the place to start with a young woman. She is ready not just to read, but to think and discuss as well."

"I have it," said Lamprocles. "Let's start at the very beginning with how the world came to be."

"With *Theogony?*" asked Socrates.

"I'm sure you can find a copy of that in the marketplace," said Lamprocles.

"And I'll look for something by Thales, too," said Socrates. "That should keep you busy for some time."

Lamprocles proved to be a kind and capable teacher. Within days, the lines and squiggles on the paper before me turned into words and sentences filled with facts and ideas.

I read all about the creation of the Cosmos and genealogy of the gods in Hesiod's *Theogony*. My reading was slow and arduous at first, but Lamprocles remained patient. Before long, he would close his eyes and recline in the shade while I read aloud.

Sometimes I would purposefully struggle or make a mistake to see if he was even listening. He would sit up abruptly and say,

"What was that?" If I would repeat my error, he would say, "Spell it!" And then we would sound it out together.

Finally, one morning I reached the last sentence. "But now, sweet-voiced Muses of Olympus, daughters of Zeus who holds the shield of protection, sing of the company of women."

"That's it!" I shouted, and Lamprocles jumped to his feet.

"What?" he cried. "What happened?"

"That's the end of *Theogony*. I read every word!"

"Don't you think I already know that?" Lamprocles chided me. "I listened to every word, you know!"

"Well, you didn't look like you were listening," I retorted.

"I was listening," Lamprocles insisted, "but I was thinking, too."

"About what?" I asked.

"I think I know why Father wants us to read Thales next," said Lamprocles.

"Why?"

"I just realized that in *Theogony*, everything comes from absolutely nothing at all," explained Lamprocles. "But Thales says that everything comes from water."

"From water?" I asked. "How can everything come from water? What about fire? Does Thales think fire comes from water?"

"It can't really," agreed Lamprocles. "But just the idea that everything has to come from something, whatever that thing is, makes sense, doesn't it?"

"Everything comes from the gods," I said. "That's what we just read."

"Yes, but where did the gods come from?" asked Lamprocles. "Hand me that book." He laid the text on his lap and ran his fingers lightly across the words. "Here," he said. "In the beginning, Chaos came to be . . . then the Earth and then Eros, god of love."

"Everything came from Earth and Eros," I said. "Earth and Eros came from Chaos."

"But what was before Chaos?" asked Lamprocles. "Before Chaos came to be?"

"Nothing?" I asked.

"Maybe," said Lamprocles. "Or maybe something else."

12

EACH DAY BECAME a new adventure, reading to Lamprocles in the Agora. Lamprocles whittled small figurines from wood as I read and while we talked. My affection for him grew quickly beyond that I had known for my own brothers. We enjoyed the lessons and looked forward to our conversations with Socrates as we walked to and from the Agora each day.

I avoided Xanthippe easily and completely. Every evening I sat by the lamp reading the text for the next day. Leda or one of the girls would bring me my meal. Sometimes they would linger, looking with wonder at the book in my hands. I would read aloud to them until they remembered their duties and scurried away.

"You just call me if you need anything," they always said. And sometimes I would call, just to let them come back into the room and hear a little more.

I felt as though I'd been carried away to the Isles of the Blessed. My reading improved until my eyes stopped seeing letters with sounds. My mind immediately grasped the words and ideas.

I read every night until Socrates came to bed. Then I turned out the lamp and nestled in beside him to talk more about what I had read that day and what I would read to Lamprocles the next. And sometimes, while we lay in bed talking, Eros would join us, sharing with us the secret pleasures of love.

Socrates became my favorite dream. When I was with him, it didn't matter whether I was awake or asleep. I had no fear of flying, no fear of falling and no fear of dying.

Even my fear of losing Socrates subsided. With the spring came General Thrasybulus who had been exiled in Thebes. He brought many allies to overthrow the Tyrants and restore democracy in Athens. Plato's uncle Charmides and cousin Critias did not survive the coup.

I often saw Plato in the Agora. He went to great lengths to make eye contact with me, but never spoke to me directly. My heart recognized a suffering in his eyes that all of the money and all of the books in Athens could not console.

Nor could I offer comfort. It was almost as if our souls had swapped spirits. My journey was from suffering to joy, and his from joy to suffering. As Heraclitus wrote, "The road up and the road down are one and the same."

We read Heraclitus after Hesiod and Thales. Like Homer and all of the poets, Hesiod invoked the Muses to inspire his words. Thales did not. He observed nature and tried to make sense of what his five senses perceived. How he concluded that water was at the heart of everything still mystified me, though. Earth, wind, fire, water . . . how could any one of them be all?

Heraclitus was making more sense. He wrote that the only constant is change. All things flow together in a constant stream, but we can never step twice into the same stream. I was no longer stepping in the stream, fighting the current. My life was a boat floating effortlessly down a river to the sea of happiness.

My body was changing, too. My belly and breasts swelled with the joy of a new life. Socrates was the first to know. Lying in bed one night he placed his hands on my slightly protruding tummy and announced, "Myrto, we are no longer alone."

"What do you mean?" I asked.

He leaned forward and kissed my belly. "Our child," he said.

I placed my hands on his. Tears of joy filled my eyes as I experienced my very first moment of truth. There were no words. No fear. Only love.

That night I dreamed of my mother. We were planting myrtle in celebration of my birthday. Suddenly, she disappeared and I could not find her. Where we had planted myrtle, there were only ashes. I scooped up the ashes and pressed them to my heart.

When I awoke, Socrates was holding me. "What is it?" he asked.

"Just a dream," I said. I buried my head in his chest and cried. He stroked my hair and let me cry.

After the tears passed, he asked, "What are you afraid of?"

I shook my head. "Nothing. Everything. I don't know."

"There is no shame in feeling fear," said Socrates. "The courage that I felt when I joined the infantry and girded my body with the heavy armor of a hoplite vanished during my first march into battle. Fear grabbed me by the chest and shook my whole body. I could barely keep step."

"And what were you most afraid of?" I asked.

"That's the thing," said Socrates. "I was suddenly afraid of everything or nothing at all, like you just said. I did not try to pretend that I was not afraid. Instead, I asked myself—what am I most afraid of?"

"And what were you most afraid of?" I asked again. "Death?"

"No." Socrates shook his head. "I did not wish to die, but I did not fear death."

"Pain?" I asked.

"I thought that might be it," Socrates admitted. "But the stronger the pain, the shorter it endures. No point enlarging it by trying to imagine it, right?"

I nodded.

"I decided I was most afraid of dishonor," said Socrates. "How odd that the thing most likely to bring me dishonor was my fear of dishonor! When I realized the foolishness behind it, fear released me, and I was able to proceed with honor. I never once faced a soldier more terrifying than my own fear," confessed Socrates.

I sighed and kissed my husband's forehead. "Childbirth is a woman's battlefield, is it not?" Images of my mother's blood-soaked bed and death in labor remained vivid in my mind.

"You are not marching into battle alone, Myrto. I will be right here with you," Socrates promised.

"What midwife would allow the father in the same room during childbirth?" I asked.

"My mother was a midwife. When I was young, she allowed me to assist her during the birth of many babies," said Socrates. "If it comes down to me or the midwife, who will you want to stay?"

"You, Socrates," I answered. "You put the baby in there. You may as well be the one to get it out."

13

I AM NO longer just Myrto. Another life, another soul grows within me. Part of me is constantly aware of this truth; part of me cannot begin to fathom it.

I find myself watching Lamprocles, imagining him a tiny seed growing in Xanthippe. He has Socrates' feet, hands and strong shoulders. But Lamprocles' facial features are much finer; and there's no mistaking the piercing, dark eyes of Xanthippe beneath his brow.

I became obsessed with Xanthippe. The day was surely coming when I could no longer go to the Agora with Socrates and Lamprocles. *What will Xanthippe say, what will she do when she learns that I am expecting?*

I will not expose my child regardless of gender, nor will my child be raised as a slave in this household. Socrates did nothing to protect me from Xanthippe. Will he protect our child? How many years will Socrates live? Surely Lamprocles will find it in his heart to love his brother. And Xanthippe loves Lamprocles most of all.

But what if my child is a girl? Will Lamprocles love a sister? I nearly drove myself to madness in this sea of torrential thoughts.

Another moon reached its fullness and passed, but I did not speak to anyone other than Socrates about our child. I did not tell him of my fear of Xanthippe. My fear of childbirth sufficiently occupied our conversation for the time being. And if I didn't survive the birth of our child, that would certainly resolve my fear of Xanthippe.

Socrates gave me a book that Aspasia had given him decades ago. "For both my mother and me," he said.

I took the book from him and began to unroll it. "Your mother could read?" I asked.

"No, I read it to her," said Socrates.

"It's all about midwifery," I said. I sat down and spread the book open on the table before me.

Socrates nodded. "I told you. My mother was a midwife," he said, "and an excellent midwife at that."

"And you are a midwife, too?" I asked. I had never heard of a man practicing midwifery.

"I don't usually deliver actual babies," Socrates admitted. "But I'm a philosophical midwife. People conceive ideas in their minds, and I help bring those ideas to light."

"How do you do that?" I asked, still studying the book. Socrates pulled up the other chair and sat beside me.

"By asking questions," replied Socrates, "and making people think."

"Is this the book that you showed me several months ago?" I asked. "The one that looked like nothing but lines and squiggles?"

"No," said Socrates, "but you have a keen eye and a powerful memory. That book was written by the same hand as this."

"Who wrote this book?" I asked. There was no name given at the beginning, just the title, *Midwifery*.

"Theano, wife of Pythagoras, wrote the book, and their daughter made numerous copies for distribution," replied Socrates. "A former Pythagorean student sold this and many other books to Pericles. Aspasia read them all and gave two of them to me."

"May I see the other one?" I asked.

"You've seen the other one," Socrates replied. His eyes smiled like those of a boy dangling an apple just beyond the horse's mouth. I moved to his lap and wrapped my arms around his neck.

"Yes, but I couldn't read then." I pressed my forehead to his. "I want to see it again now that I can read."

"But you have this book to read first," Socrates placed a hand on my belly and held me close. "You are ripe for the subject of midwifery."

"What is the other book about?" I asked.

"What is it that you want to read about?" Socrates asked.

"I want to read about everything!" This was true. I was so enamored with reading that I would have spent all day reading lists of army supplies if those were the only words available to me.

"And so you shall," responded Socrates. "But you can't read everything in one night."

Socrates motioned toward the bed. My mind wanted to spend the whole night reading, but my body agreed with Socrates. I rolled up the book knowing that it would be there for me tomorrow. As I nestled myself into bed, Socrates extinguished the lamp and joined me.

Neither Socrates nor I mentioned the book the next morning. Lamprocles and I were reading Parmenides' poem *On Nature*, so we discussed that with Socrates as we walked to the marketplace.

"I had the pleasure of meeting Parmenides when I was a very young man," Socrates told us. "He was in his mid-sixties, about my age now, when he journeyed through Athens."

"What was he like?" Lamprocles asked.

"Very handsome and very distinguished," replied Socrates. "He arrived in time for the great festival of Athena. Amidst all of the noise and confusion, people and animals everywhere, he maintained that all is one."

"What does that mean, all is one?" I asked.

"I don't know," said Socrates. "He seemed to talk in circles. I'm hoping you and Lamprocles can study the poem together and enlighten me on the journey home."

Lamprocles and I walked through the Agora and found our favorite place near the entrance of the Acropolis. We sat next to the marble statue of the Graces carved by Socrates himself. These thinly cloaked goddesses of beauty, charm and creativity invited us to study the mysteries of nature, life and divinity.

I read the poem aloud, uninterrupted. Parmenides rides in a chariot pulled by two mares who deliver him to the gate where night meets day. The daughters of the sun welcome him warmly on their journey from darkness to light. They push back the veils from their heads and lead him through truth and appearances.

The daughters of the sun claim that despite all appearances, change is an illusion that supposes things to both be and not be. They insist all things must always genuinely be. The more I read, the more puzzled I became. I finished reading and looked to Lamprocles, whose eyes were wide with wonder.

"I think he means to contradict Heraclitus," said Lamprocles. "He talks about Being—all things whole and unchanging. But we only perceive part of the Being or part of the truth. Our varying thoughts and perceptions create the illusion of motion."

"That makes no sense to me," I said.

"I'll show you what I mean," said Lamprocles. He jumped up and ran off without another word.

I sat reading and pondering this strange poem full of paradox and riddles. The poem spoke not only of light and darkness, but also of male and female. At the center of all is the goddess who created Eros to unite male and female, a goddess of union and painful birth who mixes the seeds of Love in proper proportion, producing new well-formed bodies, both male and female.

Like the body forming in my own belly. I wanted desperately to tell Lamprocles of the child within me. I wanted us to read the midwifery book together.

Lamprocles returned with a handful of small papyrus squares, a pen and ink. On the first square of papyrus he drew a caterpillar at the bottom in the far right corner. On the second he drew the caterpillar a bit higher and further to the left. He continued drawing the caterpillar, each time a little higher and a little further left until a caterpillar appeared on each page.

When the ink had dried on the last page, he stacked them all up. "Hold them right here," he said turning the left side toward me.

I held the pages with my left hand at the top and my right hand at the bottom. "Like this?" I asked.

Lamprocles nodded. "Now watch!" Lamprocles pulled open the stack to the back piece of papyrus. He dropped one sheet after another and I watched in amazement as the caterpillar climbed to the top of the page before me.

"Did you see the caterpillar move?" Lamprocles asked, his voice trembling with excitement.

I nodded. He took the papyrus from me and spread them out in order.

"But if you look at them all at once, each remains still," he said. "The appearance of movement comes from seeing only one sheet at a time."

"The appearance of movement comes because you were moving the pages," I said.

"But that's not the point," said Lamprocles. "The point is the caterpillar seems to move. Each complete drawing becomes part of one moving caterpillar."

"Show me again," I said. We took turns holding the pieces and flipping through them until the joy of watching the caterpillar climb completely replaced my confusion about its meaning.

14

THAT EVENING WHEN Leda brought me my supper she eyed me carefully and stroked her chin. "You've got the glow about you," she said finally.

I knew instantly that she knew. "What glow?" I asked anyway.

"There's a baby coming," Leda stated with an air of authority.

"Another girl to rescue from the mountain?" I asked, still pretending I did not understand.

"Not on the mountain." Leda shook her head. "In your belly."

I neither confessed nor denied the fact. It still seemed more like a dream. Talking to Leda about it would somehow make it real.

"Have you told Mr. Socrates?" Leda asked.

I shook my head. "He told me."

Leda burst out laughing. "Who ever heard of the husband telling the wife!" Then she put her hands on her hips. "And just when were you planning to tell Mama Leda?" she scolded. "Why, you need to be eating boiled eggs and fresh fruit and drinking goat's milk."

Leda began pacing around the room, fussing and planning and scolding as if the baby were coming tomorrow. I watched her with amusement.

Finally, I worked up the courage to ask her what was really on my mind. "What do you suppose Xanthippe will say?" I asked.

Leda froze. "Well, now, that is hard to guess, isn't it?" She stared at my belly for the longest time. "Pull your tunic in tight and let me see how big you are," she instructed.

"How long has it been since you've had the blood?" she asked finally.

"Not since summer," I said.

"Then we'll have a baby come spring," Leda calculated.

I liked the way she said "we'll have a baby." Indeed, I would not march into this battle alone.

When Socrates joined me after supper, I told him how Leda had guessed that I was with child.

"You can't get much past Leda," said Socrates. "She saw it in your eyes, though, not in your belly."

"Still, I'm wondering if we should tell Lamprocles," I said.

Socrates wrapped his arms around me placing both hands on my tummy. "It's your baby," he said. "You can tell anyone you like."

"What if it's a girl?" I asked.

"Then we shall love her," replied Socrates.

"But surely you must want a son." It seemed impossible that anyone could actually want a daughter.

"I have a son," said Socrates.

"Yes, but surely you want another son," I insisted.

"Do you not want a daughter?" asked Socrates.

I did not know how to answer that question. "I am afraid to want a daughter," I finally replied.

"Why?" asked Socrates.

Inside I was screaming. *You know why! You know that people are as likely to expose a girl as they are to keep her! Don't you know what a curse it is to be a woman in this world?* Outside, I just shook my head.

"It seems like such a curse to be a woman in this world," I whispered. I felt a tear slip down my cheek.

Socrates brushed away the tear and kissed my lips. "Those who believe themselves to be cursed are cursed, men and women alike," he said, still holding my face in his hands. "I do not believe you are cursed, Myrto. Do you?"

Do I? Of course, I do! How could a woman not believe she is cursed? And yet . . . "I do not feel cursed when I am with you," I admitted.

Socrates smiled. "Then it is good that we spend so much time together." He poured himself a cup of wine. "Would you like some?"

I shook my head. "Just water will be fine."

"Then I'll add a little honey to sweeten your disposition."

Socrates swilled a mouthful of wine before swallowing. He poured me a cup of water and added a drizzle of honey. Then he poured a splash of water into the wine in his own cup. He sat down beside me and swirled his wine before taking another swallow.

I stared at the cup of water between my hands. *It is good that we spend so much time together. But everything will change when the child is born. No more marketplace. No more discussions. At least I'll still have books to read. Surely Socrates and Lamprocles will at least bring me books to read.*

"Myrto," Socrates said gently.

When I looked up I realized my eyes were full of tears.

"What is it?" asked Socrates.

I shook my head.

"You do not want to tell me?" he asked.

75

I shook my head again. *Why is it always so hard to find the words . . . and then to find the courage to say the words?*

"Do you really think that my going with you and Lamprocles to the Agora is a good thing?" I asked.

"Of course," replied Socrates. "It delights me to see you learning and growing together with Lamprocles. How could that not be a good thing?"

"It's not that it's not good," I stammered. "It's just that . . . " I could not finish the thought.

"Just what, Myrto?" Socrates set his wine on the table and moved to comfort me.

"Just that everything is changing." I struggled to get the words out.

"Are you not happy with how your life has changed?"

I shook my head. "No. I mean, I am happy with my own change, but now, with a baby . . . "

Socrates nodded. "I see. What do you think will happen with the baby?"

My shame prevented me from facing Socrates. I stood and walked to our bed. Socrates followed me.

As we lay side by side on our backs in bed, Socrates asked again. "Myrto, what do you think will happen once the baby is born?"

"I will have to go back to being just another woman," I whispered. My tears flowed freely in the darkness.

Socrates propped himself up on his elbow and rested his head on his hand. With his other hand, he reached out to me, turning me to face him. "There's no going back, Myrto," said Socrates. "We can only go forward and become who we are."

"That's easy for you to say." A bitter laugh escaped my lips. "In all of your philosophical being and becoming, you will always be a man, free to come and go as you please."

"What do you want me to do?" Socrates asked. "Do you not want our child?"

"I do want our child!" The truth of this declaration surprised me. "I do want this child," I said again. "But I know that I will have to stay home to care for the baby." I paused hoping that Socrates would say something. He did not. "I do not want to be trapped here without you," I whispered.

"Trapped?" asked Socrates. He paused. "Myrto, what is it that you are most afraid of?"

I took a deep breath and summoned the courage to tell my husband the truth. "Xanthippe," I replied.

Socrates laughed. I pushed him away and rolled over on my back. "Please don't be angry," Socrates said, still laughing. "I'm laughing at my own foolishness, not at you."

I do feel angry. Angry and hurt. I said nothing.

"I thought that you were going to tell me that you're afraid of death," said Socrates. "Your death, the death of our child, or maybe even the death of this old man."

Am I really more afraid of Xanthippe than of death? And Socrates' death would leave both me and my child without a home. Am I the foolish one here? I turned back to face Socrates and put my hand on his side. "I really am afraid of Xanthippe," I confessed.

Socrates laughed again, but this time I did not feel hurt. "Let me tell you a secret," said Socrates, "but you must promise never to tell a soul." He wrapped his arms around me and held me close.

"I promise," I said.

Socrates whispered in my ear. "Xanthippe is afraid of you."

15

XANTHIPPE IS AFRAID of me. This new thought completely possessed me. The words sang over and over in my mind as we walked to the Agora the next morning. *Xanthippe is afraid of me.* The idea was absurd. I found myself covering my mouth with my hand to stifle the giggles.

Xanthippe was afraid of nothing. She did not fear Socrates. The image of Xanthippe dumping the chamber pot on Socrates' head stayed with me. *Xanthippe is afraid of me. Xanthippe is afraid of nothing. I am nothing.* Yet as we crossed the river on our path to the city, I did not feel like nothing. There was something inside me—alive and growing.

Xanthippe is afraid of me. The thought continued to amuse me greatly. I began to reconsider my own fears. What else was I afraid of? Was I not still afraid of what the future might hold, especially when Socrates dies? Afraid of giving birth? Afraid of being trapped in Xanthippe's house once my child was born while Socrates and Lamprocles continue spending their days in the Agora without me?

Xanthippe is afraid of me. I must have laughed aloud.

"What's so funny?" Lamprocles asked.

"Nothing," I said. I shook my head, but my lips formed a smile. I was surprised to see that we had passed the last belt of olive trees outside the city wall.

Socrates took my hand. "Lamprocles and I were just discussing what the two of you might study next."

"Everyone's talking about Protagoras and Gorgias. They can use logic and reason to prove or disprove anything you like," said Lamprocles.

"What's the point of that?" I asked.

Lamprocles stopped and crossed his arms. "The point is to become a more excellent and persuasive public speaker," Lamprocles retorted. "This is the most useful skill in a democracy; wouldn't you agree, Father?"

"Public speaking does seem to be important," Socrates replied. Without releasing my hand, he touched Lamprocles' elbow. "But I wonder why it is so important."

Once again we were walking together.

"It distinguishes those who lead from those who follow," insisted Lamprocles. "Those who can persuade best direct the course of public opinion."

Socrates sighed. "Perhaps the public is too easily persuaded."

We passed through the gate and into the city. Lamprocles made his way through the crowd toward the marketplace and was soon out of our sight. Socrates kept hold of my hand through the hustling and pushing. We nestled in the wake of a sturdy slave girl, gracefully carrying her pitcher on her head. When she reached a fountain on the next street corner, I watched her reach her hand into the cool, gushing water. I stopped for a drink as well. A pair of schoolboys scurried past us, writing tablets in hand, each trying to out stride the other.

House doors opened, and the masters stepped into the street, accompanied by sons and servants. I was the only wife. Just me. Yet with Socrates holding me close and our child in my belly, I did not feel alone or out of place. I took a deep breath and imagined Xanthippe, heavy with Lamprocles, in my stead. *Xanthippe is afraid of me.* I laughed. Socrates looked over at me and smiled.

Lamprocles was waiting for us beneath our favorite bay tree in the market place. I felt Lamprocles' dark eyes staring heavily upon me as we approached. The eyes of Xanthippe. *Perhaps Lamprocles is afraid of me as well.* This thought carried a wave of sadness. I made myself a seat in the grass beside him and wished that he felt closer.

It was time to tell him about the baby.

"Forgive me, Lamprocles, if I do not seem quite myself today," I began. "My thoughts were not in our conversation this morning, but on something that I've wanted to tell you from the moment I learned."

Socrates had seated himself directly before us both. Lamprocles looked at him searchingly, then looked back to me.

"What is it?" Lamprocles implored, leaning forward. I looked at Socrates, who nodded that I should proceed.

I struggled to my feet and pulled my tunic tight around my growing belly.

Lamprocles eyes brightened, and he leapt to his feet. "A baby!" he shouted.

Tears of relief and joy filled my eyes and flowed down my cheeks. I nodded.

"When?" asked Lamprocles, turning to Socrates. "When will the baby arrive?"

"The baby will come with the spring," replied Socrates. The words were simple, but the love in his voice was as profound as that of Demeter anticipating the annual return of her daughter Persephone from Hades. I wiped the tears from my eyes.

Lamprocles again turned his gaze toward my belly, his eyes filled with wonder. "There really is a child growing inside you."

I nodded and reached for his hand, placing it gently on my stomach. "Your brother or sister."

"My brother or sister," Lamprocles repeated. Then, as these words seemed to sink in, Lamprocles withdrew his hand and furrowed his brow. "Does Mother know about this?"

I shook my head. Fear seized me.

"I don't know," replied Socrates.

"You haven't told her?" asked Lamprocles.

"No, but she may have guessed," said Socrates. "Or Leda may have told her."

"You told Leda?" This was an accusation, not a question.

"Lamprocles, Leda guessed it herself only last night," I responded quietly.

Lamprocles still looked hurt. "So you've told no one?" he asked Socrates.

"Only Myrto," Socrates said with a laugh.

Lamprocles looked puzzled. "Father told you?"

I nodded and shrugged my shoulders.

"How did you know?" Lamprocles asked. Without waiting for a response, he turned to me and asked, "How can the man who professes to know nothing, be the first to know anything?"

Socrates' eyes twinkled. "By knowing I know nothing. Others see what they think they know and miss what really is right before us all."

Lamprocles did not seem to hear this. "When will you tell Mother?" he asked. "How will you tell her?"

Socrates shrugged. "Your mother will know when she wants to know. She doesn't need me to tell her anything."

At that moment, a group of young men called from a short distance, "Good morning, Socrates!" We exchanged greetings as they approached. Lamprocles looked at me and motioned south toward the Acropolis. I nodded.

"If you'll excuse us, Father, Myrto and I are going to walk up to the Acropolis and finish our discussion about what to study next."

The young men bade us a polite goodbye, but seemed eager to have Socrates' full attention.

Lamprocles and I walked in silence along the Panathenaic Way past the Hill of Ares. It seemed a long walk for such a short distance. When we arrived at the statue of the Graces, Lamprocles finally broke the silence.

"What does it feel like," he asked, "to have a child growing inside you?"

I placed both hands on my belly. "It feels very strange and very wonderful," I replied. "I also feel very tired sometimes."

Lamprocles immediately took my hand and found a place where we could sit comfortably. "Can you feel the baby moving inside you?" he asked once we were settled.

"Not yet," I replied. My mind carried me back to my childhood to a faint memory just before my mother's death. "I remember putting my hand on my mother's belly when her time was near and feeling the baby punch and kick. Once I even saw the movement."

"Was it a boy or a girl?" asked Lamprocles.

"A boy," I said softly.

"I didn't know that you have a younger brother, too."

I shook my head. "He died at birth." I paused. "And mother went with him," I said, my voice barely a whisper. Tears filled my eyes. I could not stop them. I did not want to stop them. They streamed down my cheeks.

Lamprocles looked frightened. He took my hand. "How old were you?" he asked.

"Twelve."

After a long silence, Lamprocles said, "I don't want you to die, Myrto."

I gave him a hug. His acceptance of me and my child might mean a safe place for both of us eventually if Socrates were to die and Lamprocles were old enough to be the head of the household. And brave enough to stand up to Xanthippe. I pushed these thoughts from my mind and focused on the present.

"Would you be willing to read a book on midwifery with me?"

"What book?" he asked.

"A book by Theano, wife of Pythagoras. Your father has it at home."

Lamprocles nodded. "Let's study that next."

16

I COULD HARDLY contain my excitement as we walked to the Agora the next morning, Theano's book in Lamprocles' satchel.

"Father, tell me about your mother Phaenarete," Lamprocles inquired.

"Ah," Socrates responded with a knowing smile. "She was a woman of wisdom, but she would have loved and indulged you beyond measure."

"When did she die?" I asked.

"Soon after Xanthippe and I married," answered Socrates. "My father Sophroniscus died long before we were married. Neither of them lived to see the birth of their first grandson." He smiled at Lamprocles.

"That's because you waited until you were 50 years old to marry!" Lamprocles laughed. "I was lucky to be born at all."

I wondered whose idea it was to name Lamprocles after Xanthippe's father rather than Socrates' own father, Sophroniscus. Despite the warmth of our conversation, I shivered in the chilly morning air. Our walks became increasingly brisk as the days grew shorter and the sun ceased to be an early riser. Socrates must have noticed because he removed his own cloak and wrapped it around my shoulders.

"Why didn't you become a sculptor like your father?" I asked. "Your marble statue of the Graces stands as a testimony to your talent."

Socrates chuckled. "That was truly a gift to my father before he died. Sophroniscus could look at any amorphous hunk of stone and see a beautiful being, a living form within."

"And you?" I asked. I could feel heat radiating from Socrates' body to mine, even though I was bundled and he was barefoot and wearing nothing but a light tunic.

"My father trained me in the family business when I was young, but I never had his vision for sculpting," confessed Socrates.

Lamprocles nodded in my direction. "Mother says more often than not Father seemed compelled to chisel and pound away until nothing remained but a pile of dust and gravel."

"I'm afraid it's true, my dear," Socrates agreed. He drew me in even closer to the radiating warmth of his body. "I did a little better when my father at least told me what he envisioned for the stone as he did with the Graces, but we all knew that I wasn't born to be a sculptor."

"What were you born to be?" I asked, ready to pursue this topic further. But we had reached Piraeus Gate, marking the end of our morning walk and our entrance into the city.

"Father is a born lover of wisdom," offered Lamprocles before our conversation vanished in the crowd. Socrates did not disagree.

At Lamprocles' urging, we left Socrates in the Agora and walked toward the Parthenon. But we did not stop at the Parthenon. We continued walking south with the sun rising over our left shoulders, leaving Socrates and the crowds far behind.

"Where are we going?" I asked. My mind remained fixed on the book in Lamprocles' satchel, and I was anxious to begin our studies.

Lamprocles responded in verse reminiscent of Homer's *Hymn to Artemis:*

When Artemis is satisfied
Her huntress heart well-cheered
She journeys to her brother's house
And slackens her great bow.
Oh, Muse! Oh, Grace! It's time to dance
With her dear Twin Apollo.

"What's that supposed to mean?" I asked impatiently.

"It means that if we are to study midwifery, we must find a place pleasing to Artemis," said Lamprocles. "The Acropolis is a place for men. We must seek out another place—a place of women, inspiration and wild beasts." He pointed to the pine-green Hills of the Muses. "There."

We walked in silence to the very top of the tallest hill and found a small clearing that overlooked the Parthenon. Finally, Lamprocles removed the book from his satchel and handed it to me. "Now," he said, "let's read."

I began. We did nothing but read the whole day through. We read reverently without discussion, taking turns whenever one voice grew weak. A growing sense of wonder engulfed me as we read about the mysteries of the female body and the miracles of life and healing.

Theano showed no disrespect for the gods, yet they were oddly absent from the actual cause or cure for illness, injury and disease.

Hygeia, Panacea and Iaso, goddesses of cleanliness, prevention and healing, responded to all equally. There were no stories about how Apollo saved their father Asclepius by cutting open the womb of Koronis or how Asclepius grew in the art of medicine, using the sacred power of snakes for healing.

Nor was it all about the female body and childbirth. There was a strange mixture of male and female and the body's own healing power when kept clean and properly nourished. I studied Lamprocles' body as he read and marveled at how his hands held the book for his eyes to see and his mind to comprehend and his mouth to voice the words aloud. Each part worked together as a whole with such natural ease. It was no harder, really, to accept that each of us holds within us the ability to re-balance the four humors of blood, black bile, yellow bile, and phlegm.

We read about using citrus to reduce phlegm, how the crushed leaves of lemon balm can be rubbed on the skin to repel insects or brewed into a relaxing tea. We read that dry treatment of wounds is best, and we should only use water or wine to clean wounds when absolutely necessary. We learned the importance of keeping our fingernails trimmed and clean and the meanings of different fevers, pains and excretions. We began to understand the implications of subtle changes in complexion, movement and pulse and the value of keen observation.

Both light and darkness shimmered in each word, with shadows looming behind every moment of enlightenment. The book told of the need to survey carefully the patient's environment and to listen closely to all family history. Theano even recommended measuring a patient's pulse as she talks to discern when she is lying. There were instructions on using pessaries of lemon, pomegranate, fig and even sea sponges to preserve the honor of a mistress and pre-vent the birth of a child.

In the end, Lamprocles did much more reading, and I did much more listening. He devoured the book with voracious appetite while I quietly opened my heart to its meaning. The text answered question after question I'd never thought to ask, and when that first day was done, we had not even begun to learn about childbirth itself. We did, however, make a pact to memorize, recite and keep the oath that Theano required for all midwives:

"I swear by Apollo, Asclepius, Hygeia, Panacea and Iaso to keep according to my ability the following oath: I will consider dear to me as my parents she who taught me the art of midwifery. I will look upon her children as my own sisters and teach them this art."

"I will never do harm to anyone, but will act for the good of my patients according to my ability and judgment. I will preserve the purity of my life and art."

"In every house where I come, I will enter only for the good of my patient, keeping myself far from all intentional ill-doing and all seduction. All that may come to my knowledge through the exercise of midwifery which ought not to be spread abroad, I will keep secret and never reveal."

"I will keep this oath faithfully so that I may enjoy my life and the practice of my art, respected by all for all times."

As we descended from the Hill of Muses, I breathed in the cleansing odor of pines. Lamprocles and I were not merely stepson and stepmother or simply fellow students in the art of midwifery. We had sworn an oath that would forever bind us together as brother and sister in the eyes of Apollo and Artemis.

17

WE RETURNED TO the Hill of Muses day after day to study midwifery. The earth awakened from her slumber, and winter's cool dampness faded away. As our studies moved from general health into graphic details of labor and childbirth, Lamprocles insisted that we discuss every sentence in depth. At times we would spend an hour on the meaning of one word. There are countless ways for things to go wrong during the actual birthing; I died a thousand deaths in my heart as we read about each one of them.

Some parts were comforting, however. For example, the midwife should ask the woman what she believes will help. "Do not argue with her or attempt to dissuade her. Always acknowledge her requests and address her concerns. It is more important that she believes you are doing as she asks than to actually do it, especially when the requested treatment would be particularly odorous, bloody or dirty."

This idea appealed to me. "What do you suppose she means by that?" I interrupted as Lamprocles read.

"Hold on, she's going to tell us," he replied impatiently and continued reading. "There is no value to using earthworms, powdered sow's dung, canine placentas, newborn goat membranes or spider webs during labor and delivery. It is better to keep the birthing area clean."

"Thank you, Hygeia!" I said, leaning over Lamprocles shoulder to read this wonderful passage with my own eyes.

Lamprocles laughed. "Yes," he agreed. "We should give thanks to the goddess of cleanliness!"

Gradually each new fear subsided more quickly until my entire well of fears ran dry. I began to enjoy our discussions again. I would not be at the mercy of an inexpert midwife and her foul treatments. I had choices. I could kneel or stand or squat on my heels or sit in a birthing chair, whatever felt most comfortable to me. Socrates would surely honor my wishes.

"Do you suppose Socrates still has Phaenarete's birthing chair?" I asked.

"I don't know that she ever owned one," Lamprocles replied. "And if Father has it, I've never seen it."

"I'm sure you never looked for it," I teased.

"And I'm sure I would remember a chair with a big hole in the center of it whether I was looking for it or not!" Lamprocles shot back.

I noticed my back and shoulders were growing stiff from sitting for such a long time. As I struggled to my feet, Lamprocles set the book aside and jumped up to help me.

"I just need to walk around a bit," I said, grasping my shoulder with my hand and stretching my neck.

"That's good," Lamprocles nodded. "Walking is good. So is massage. Would you like me to massage your neck and shoulders?"

I laughed. "I know, I know. A healthy, well-nourished mother-to-be should take regular walks and receive relaxing massages to avoid complications during delivery." I continued walking and stretching. "I'll ask Leda or Socrates to massage my belly and back with warm olive oil when we return this evening."

"The baby will be less likely to drop in a breech position." Lamprocles reminded me. The larger I got, the more serious Lamprocles became, but the more inclined I was toward laughter.

The text completely entranced Lamprocles, but his focus remained on my body and the child inside me. He wanted to be sure we knew what to do under all circumstance. Regardless of the complications, he was determined to learn every appropriate response to save me and the baby.

According to Theano, first births are the most difficult because women are often bound up with fear. By the second birth, a woman at least knows in her own heart that she can survive. I suppose I should have already known that having survived my own birth and seeing the multitudes of people in the world. It just never occurred to me to face the fear and release it rather than resisting it and encouraging it to grow stronger.

As we continued, I began to think Lamprocles was more afraid than I. All that changed late one afternoon as we were nearing completion of the book. The anticipation pushed me to read more and talk less.

"You're going too fast," Lamprocles complained when I refused to pause after every word. "Let me read today."

Lamprocles clearly did not want the book to end. I lay down in the grass and propped my head on his satchel as a pillow. *Why am I in such a hurry?* As I relaxed and listened to Lamprocles' many commentaries as he read, I realized that it wasn't the book I wanted to finish. I was finally ready for my child to be born. As I drifted along, lost in my own thoughts of holding and nurturing the baby, Lamprocles gave a shout that nearly sent me into labor.

"Myrto!" he exclaimed. "Listen to this: 'A midwife must be a person of sympathetic disposition, but need not have borne a child.'"

I sat up just enough to see him. Still leaning back on my elbows and feeling totally bewildered, I shook my head. "So," I paused trying to grasp his meaning. "A midwife doesn't actually have to be a mother herself as long as she's sympathetic."

Lamprocles was on his feet, pacing excitedly. "Not a woman!" he proclaimed. "A person! A sympathetic person!" He was jumping around so much I couldn't follow his body or his thoughts.

"Myrto, if you do away with the requirement of having personally given birth, a midwife could be a man!" He was dancing around me in pure delight. "I know that Father has always considered himself a philosophical midwife of men, helping to labor through their thoughts and give birth to great ideas, but I always thought that no man could truly, literally be a midwife."

He stopped dancing and sat beside me. He reached out his hand and lifted me gently up to face him. I nodded as his words sank in. "Socrates and I have already discussed that I would rather have him with me when our child is born than the most experienced midwife in the city."

Lamprocles face fell, and he turned slightly away so I could no longer see his eyes. "Well, yes, of course, Father," he stammered. In the silence of his long pause, I suddenly understood. Still I waited to be certain.

Lamprocles faced me and held my hands in earnest. "Myrto, except for my own parents, you are more dear to me than anyone. The child you are carrying is my sister or brother. If Father were to agree, would you . . . " He faltered. *Surely no man has ever asked to be a midwife. Not in Hesiod or Homer, Parmenides or even Pythagoras who considered all men and women to be equal. The words simply do not exist.*

I nodded. I had already weathered a thousand births with Lamprocles. His presence through the next one would ensure the survival of us all.

"Do you want to ask him or shall I?" Lamprocles asked.

"Let's ask him together."

Lamprocles nodded and handed me the book. "Here," he said. "Let's finish reading first."

18

AS WE WALKED home that evening, Lamprocles immediately engaged Socrates in a conversation regarding Phaenarete's work as a midwife.

"In truth," said Socrates, "I found my mother's work much more intriguing than my father's work as a sculptor."

"Did you ever wish you could go with her and watch her work?" asked Lamprocles.

"Oh, yes," replied Socrates. Lamprocles gave me a smile and a nod as Socrates continued, "On more than one occasion as a child, I had the opportunity to watch my mother work and to witness the elusive nature of life itself."

"The husband did not object?" I asked.

"No," said Socrates. "I was still a young boy." He laughed heartily. "I didn't realize it at the time, but I suppose they thought I was just some slave boy there to carry the tools of my master."

"What did you witness?" asked Lamprocles. His eyes widened with anticipation, and I could see that he was much encouraged by the fact that his father had attended more than one birth when he was young.

"I saw children entering this world, wrapped in human flesh, such perfect little people with all of their tiny body parts." Socrates stopped walking and stared into the clouds, transfixed as though he were actually looking back in time. "I watched my mother hold her own breath, waiting for that first breath of the child to erupt into a cry announcing to the world that a new life had indeed begun."

He looked back at Lamprocles. "There is a moment when you really can't be sure. Sometimes a perfect little creature with all of its visible body parts in place arrives, but never takes that first breath of life."

I nodded. That was my brother Acheron. I shuddered with the memory of that midwife, covered in my mother's blood, holding the lifeless baby boy. Socrates turned to me as if to comfort me and said, "It's not up to us, you know. Some carry the gift of life within themselves and some do not."

We continued walking, but at a slower, more contemplative pace. "Of course, my interest in my mother's work leaned less toward medical extraction and more toward the emergence and development of a separate being, a living soul."

I could feel the conversation shifting from midwifery to philosophy. Socrates continued talking, completely unaware of where Lamprocles and I wanted to go with this discussion. "If this new person has the gift of life, and the gift of life is good, then what might this person do to develop this inherent goodness?" Socrates asked.

Lamprocles kept looking at me, raising his eyebrows and mouthing the word, "Ask!"

"Did your mother have a birthing chair?" I asked Socrates. Lamprocles scowled and shook his head.

"As a matter of fact, she did," Socrates replied. "It was a lovely wooden chair with a carving of Artemis on the back and arm rests in the shape of the letter *pi.*"

"Whatever became of it?" I asked.

Socrates was facing me and couldn't see Lamprocles pointing to himself and silently mouthing, "Ask about me."

Socrates shrugged. "It's been so long ago, my dear, I really don't know. She probably gave it to one of her favorite apprentices."

"After all that Lamprocles and I have read, I think I should like to use a birthing chair as I labor." I motioned to Lamprocles to be patient.

"That's a wonderful idea," said Socrates. "I'm sure we can find one if we put our minds to the task."

"Theano suggests that a birthing chair requires two assistants to support each of the woman's arms while the midwife catches the baby," I continued. "I told Lamprocles that we had already agreed that you would help deliver the baby, but we'll still need two assistants."

Socrates was smiling as he looked at me and then Lamprocles and then back to me. He put his arm around my waist and rested his hand on the side of my bulging middle. "That is an excellent point," he finally replied. "Do you have anyone in mind that you would like to assist us?"

I heard Lamprocles draw in a deep breath and hold it.

"I do," I replied. "If Lamprocles would agree, I should very much like for him to assist. I have no mother and no sisters. Lamprocles is my dearest friend. Together we have sworn to uphold the midwife's oath."

Socrates turned to Lamprocles, whose entire body suddenly filled with animation. "Myrto has asked that you assist in the birth of your brother or sister. As your father, I cannot ask you to do that."

I could feel my own eyes welling up with tears. Lamprocles remained silent, his pleading eyes fixed on his father.

Socrates cleared his throat. "As I was saying, you are under no obligation to do this, and I am not asking you as your father. But man to man, I would ask you to consider my wife's request seriously, knowing that I would humbly accept this as a great personal favor from you to me."

"Oh, Father!" Lamprocles nearly shouted. "I am honored by Myrto's request. I would be delighted to assist you both!"

Lamprocles seemed to gallop along beside us, chattering about all that needed to be done and who should do it. "I can begin making a birthing chair tomorrow." He looked me up and down. "I'll make it the perfect size just for Myrto . . . out of a horse chestnut tree. I'll sand it smooth as silk and carve not only Artemis, but Hygeia, Panacea and Iosa, too!"

Lamprocles danced over by my side. "Myrto, while I'm working on the chair, you can make bandages to swaddle the baby. And we can send the girls down to the sea to collect soft sponges." Looking back to Socrates, he asked, "Should we have Leda prepare some flower water and rose oil?"

Socrates gave him a nod as he chuckled. "All good ideas as we prepare for the glorious event." Socrates pulled me close and whispered in my ear. "I can see who's in charge here." Turning back to Lamprocles, he asked, "And what would you have me do?"

"Of course, you can help me with the chair," said Lamprocles, "but . . . when was the last time you actually read Theano's midwifery book?"

"I guess it has been a few years," admitted Socrates. He winked at me before turning back to Lamprocles, "How old are you?"

"That's what I thought!" Lamprocles exclaimed. "I can direct you to the parts that I think are most critical, so you don't have to re-read the whole thing."

"Is that all?" Socrates inquired.

Lamprocles silently counted on his fingers all of the things he'd suggested. "That's all I can think of right now," he replied.

"Aren't you two forgetting something?" Socrates asked. I loved how his eyes twinkled when he pushed us to think further.

"What?" asked Lamprocles. Then after a moment he added, "I think the two of you should choose the name."

"I agree with you there," said Socrates.

I nodded. "We also need to decide who will be supporting my other arm."

"Oh, right," said Lamprocles. "Who else do you want to help you, Myrto?

I looked from Lamprocles to Socrates. "I don't know," I confessed. "But I think it should be a woman—one who has given birth herself."

Lamprocles and Socrates nodded their agreement.

"Someone sympathetic," added Lamprocles, "with clean, well-trimmed fingernails."

19

THAT EVENING, LAMPROCLES asked Leda to massage my back and belly with warm olive oil. As her warm, strong hands worked to relax my muscles, I found myself wondering about all the work her hands had done through the years.

"Leda, how long have you been a slave?" I asked.

"My mother was a slave, so I was born a slave," she replied. She poured more oil on her hands and rubbed them together vigorously to generate additional heat.

I continued my questioning. "How long have you been with Socrates?"

"Since he and Mrs. Xanthippe married," she said. She continued massaging as I lay comfortably on my back. "I've been with Mrs. Xanthippe since she was just a week old."

I had never considered that Leda's loyalty might run much stronger to Xanthippe than to Socrates.

"I'm afraid your belly's too big for you to just roll over. Can you roll onto your side a bit so I can work on your back?"

I rolled over as far as my protruding middle allowed. "How old were you then?" I asked.

"About your age, Mrs. Myrto," Leda responded, "maybe a little younger."

"So they got you to help care for Xanthippe when she was a baby?" I suddenly missed Timo. My brothers had never offered to send her with me when I married Socrates. Perhaps if Bion had been a girl, they would have allowed me to keep her. *A woman who has given birth!* I tried to picture Timo in my mind. More than a year had passed since I last saw her. *Would Socrates and Lamprocles approve?*

I realized I knew nothing about Timo's life prior to Father buying her. She knew everything about me, but I had never thought to ask her about herself or Bion's father or anything.

Leda continued working, firmly and methodically. I wanted her to tell me more.

"So where did you live before that?" I asked.

She motioned for me to roll over to my other side. "You surely do have a lot of questions." Leda laughed. "Why would you want to know so much about Old Mama Leda all of the sudden?" she asked.

"I'm just interested," I said. "You're the only woman I ever talk to, but I don't really know anything about you."

"I suppose that's so," Leda agreed. Her hands slowed a bit, and she began using her thumbs to massage around my shoulder blade. "Still, I don't know what to tell you."

"Tell me everything," I suggested.

Leda laughed. "If I was to tell you everything, you'd be as old as I am, and I'd be dead!"

I laughed, too. I was feeling so relaxed. "Then tell me this," I said. "Were you there when Lamprocles was born?"

"Oh, yes, ma'am."

My eyes were closed, but I could feel her nodding as her hands continued their work.

"After the midwife was sure that little Mr. Lamprocles was fine, I cleaned him up while she tended to Mrs. Xanthippe." Genuine affection filled her voice when she said both Lamprocles' and Xanthippe's names.

I turned this over in my mind until an entirely new thought burst forth. I sat up on the bed. "Leda," I said, "have you ever had a baby?"

Leda stopped massaging and just stared at me. Finally, she nodded. A tear crept through the corner of her eye. I reached for hand and pulled her toward me, motioning for her to sit beside me. I held her hand in mine and studied the deep creases on her palm and the protruding bones and veins on the back. The scars from years of nicks and cuts glistened with oil.

I reached for her other hand and held them both. The kind and gentle hands that had just massaged my belly held Lamprocles the day that he was born and had even cradled Xanthippe when she was a baby. These hands had cleaned and fed every baby girl that Xanthippe rescued from exposure. I smiled. Despite many years of hard work, Leda kept her fingernails clean and well-trimmed.

"How many babies have you had?" I asked quietly.

"Two." Leda sighed deeply. "So long ago," she whispered.

I wondered who the father might have been and what had become of them. Slaves could not marry. Their children belonged to the master to do with as he pleased. "Boys or girls?" I asked.

Lena shrugged. "I never saw either one."

"The midwife didn't even tell you whether you had a boy or a girl?" I asked.

"There was no midwife. Just another slave. She said it's better not to know."

"And the father," I wondered aloud, "what became of him?"

"The master's sons," Leda replied. "The youngest married shortly before the second child was born. The day after I gave birth my master sold me to Mr. Lamprocles, Mrs. Xanthippe's father. They needed a wet nurse for the baby."

We sat for a moment in silence. "And that's how you became Mama Leda," I said. She nodded and rose to her feet.

"Wait, Mama Leda." I scooted my belly to the end of the bed, put my feet on the floor and pushed myself up with both hands. "There's one more thing I want to ask you."

Leda turned back to me, her eyes filled with apprehension. She took a deep breath and waited.

"Do you think Xanthippe would mind terribly if you assisted with the birth of my baby?"

Leda's breath exploded with an, "Oh!" I'd never seen such a look of surprise on anyone's face.

"We've decided not to call the midwife," I explained. "Socrates wants to deliver the baby himself, and Lamprocles is going to assist. He's going to make a birthing chair and support me on one side. I need someone else to support me on the other."

Leda just stood there, taking it all in.

"I would really like to have a woman there with me, too. Someone who has survived childbirth herself. You, Leda. I really want you to be there with me."

A rush of maternal love swallowed us both up for a moment.

"I'll be with you, child," Leda whispered.

I gave her a big hug. "Thank you, Mama Leda."

She leaned her shoulders over my protruding belly and reached her sturdy arms around me. Before she let go, Leda added, "You'll just have to ask Mrs. Xanthippe, that's all."

20

JUST ASK MRS. Xanthippe. Hestia, Artemis and Athena! There must be another way. Socrates should be the one to ask her. Yes, that would be much better. Socrates can ask.

When Socrates came to bed, I kissed his hand. "I would like for Mama Leda to be the one who assists us along with Lamprocles during the birth of our child," I told him.

He placed his hand on my belly and nestled his warm body in next to mine. "An excellent choice, my dear."

"I'm glad you think so." I smiled in the darkness. "Leda has agreed, but I suppose you'll need to ask Xanthippe."

Socrates chuckled softly. "You want me to ask Xanthippe?"

"Yes, I do," I replied. "Why does that strike you as funny? It certainly wouldn't be appropriate for Leda to ask."

"Why not?" asked Socrates. He scooted over a bit and sat up in bed.

"She is a slave," I replied. "She cannot be the one to make the request, and she cannot assist without first obtaining permission from Xanthippe."

"So you've talked to Leda?" asked Socrates.

"Yes."

"And what exactly did she say?" asked Socrates.

"That she would be with me, but that someone would have to talk to Xanthippe," I replied.

"Someone?" Socrates pressed further. "Did she suggest who that someone might be?"

"Us," I replied curtly. "You, me . . . I don't know. Are you afraid to ask her?"

"No," Socrates responded firmly. "Are you?"

I took a deep breath. "You know I am," I said.

"Why?" asked Socrates. "What are you afraid of? That she'll say no? She can say no just as easily to me. Probably even more easily."

I sighed. "You're right. Maybe we should have Lamprocles ask. She would be less likely to refuse him."

"You would place Lamprocles in a position where he must choose between you and his own mother?" Socrates waited, but I did not respond. He again lay beside me and took me into his arms. "Why don't you ask her yourself?"

"I just told you," I said. The words choked in my throat. "I am afraid."

"I know," Socrates reassured me. "But you do not have to give fear control of your actions."

I could only shake my head. Tears streamed down my cheeks and onto Socrates' chest. He held me close until I fell into a deep sleep.

The next morning, Lamprocles went to work on the birthing chair while Socrates read quietly nearby, ready to lend a hand whenever Lamprocles requested.

I was sitting in the courtyard preparing bandages when Xanthippe walked briskly past me and out into the street. My heart pounded in my chest, but I rose to my feet and followed her.

"Xanthippe," I called. "Please wait."

Xanthippe spun around, her eyes shooting incredulous arrows into my soul.

"Why are you following me?" she hissed.

"I need to ask you something," I said. "Please." I approached slowly, fixing my gaze upon hers and reminding myself that her eyes were no different than Lamprocles' dark, sparkling eyes. Eyes that once belonged to an infant who surely gazed deeply into Leda's eyes while nursing.

"What is it?" Xanthippe asked sharply.

"I will have the baby soon," I started.

"That's quite apparent," she retorted. "You are no doubt praying for a son. Not even Artemis would save a girl who looks like Socrates from exposure."

I felt myself bristling. *Do not respond with an equally cutting remark. Let the anger go. Lamprocles loves this woman. Leda loves this woman. Feel their love.*

I slowly dropped to my knees before her. "I am here to ask that you permit Leda to assist me during the birth." I looked up at her, hands beneath my belly in my lap, humbly awaiting her reply.

Xanthippe cocked her head in disbelief. Her eyes narrowed, and her lips scowled. "You would ask a favor of me?"

I nodded.

"Why should I show you any favor? I owe you no favors." Her voice remained gruff, but there was a subtle softening in her stance.

Again I nodded. "You are right. You owe me no favors. So I ask not for myself but for my child, a child who has done you no wrong, the half-brother or sister of your beloved Lamprocles."

Xanthippe drew herself up straight and put her hands on her hips. "Why do you want Leda?" she asked, her eyes still glaring. "You'll have the midwife. That is enough."

I lowered my gaze and shook my head. "No," I said. "There will be no midwife. Socrates intends to deliver the child himself."

"You must be joking!" cried Xanthippe. "He's an even bigger fool than I thought." She slapped her knees and stared at me in wonder.

I remained silent, not wishing to agree or disagree with her.

"Stand up," she commanded. I struggled awkwardly to my feet. "You may borrow Leda and whatever luck she can bring you." She continued to look me over, assessing the size of the child and my own breadth and girth. "And in the unlikely event that you should survive the birth of your child, you will owe me a favor."

I nodded. "I will owe you a favor." Inside I felt a sudden flash of light followed by a soul-piercing crash of thunder. *What favor? What have I agreed to do?*

Xanthippe smelled my fear and smiled.

I struggled to regain my composure. "I will do you a favor, but you must know that I will do no harm to anyone."

Xanthippe laughed spitefully. "Oh, yes," she said, rolling her head back and savoring her triumph. "You are quite harmless, aren't you?"

"I am quite serious," I replied evenly.

"You think you're so much better than other women?" Xanthippe growled. "Young, beautiful granddaughter of Aristides the Just. Reading and talking philosophy every day. Just you wait. Wait until that child wants out, and you'll see you're no different than every other woman . . . you'll be grunting and panting and groaning. Just you wait."

I shuddered. I felt the baby turn over inside me. But instead of picturing myself in labor, I pictured Xanthippe, grunting and straining to give birth to Lamprocles. I pictured Leda, young and brawny, giving birth to a baby she never even got to hold. And holding Xanthippe instead. And loving her.

"You're right," I said, looking directly into the blackness of her eyes and seeing a faint reflection of myself. "I am no different than you."

Xanthippe's mouth dropped open just a bit. I couldn't tell if she was surprised or if she meant to say something, but no words came out. She turned abruptly, and walked away.

As I stood and watched her go, a tremendous sense of strength filled my body. I cradled my belly and felt a tingling surge from the top of my head to my heart that radiated into my arms and legs. "We're going to be fine," I said. "We're going to be just fine."

21

SOPHRONISCUS ARRIVED WITH the first new moon of spring. He was a strapping young boy, born with clear blue eyes that grew darker with each sunrise. He seldom cried during his first month for he was always cradled in my arms, or the loving arms of Socrates, Lamprocles or Leda. Somehow my body responded to his hearty appetite, producing enough milk to feed a small herd of goats. At the end of each day, we nestled Sophroniscus between us in our bed. He drew warmth from Socrates and nourishment from me throughout the night.

Before long, Socrates returned to the Agora, and Lamprocles began training in the gymnasium outside the city walls to strengthen his body for competition in the public games and for military service. Though part of me missed my days with them, I spent most of each day lost in Sophroniscus' sweet gaze or wondering at the gentle rise and fall of his chest when his eyes closed. As the season changed from spring to summer, I began taking walks along the River Illisus. Leda fashioned an old tunic of Lamprocles into a pouch to wear around my neck and cradle Sophroniscus. He could sleep, eat or look around as he wished, while I walked comfortably.

I pretended I was Sappho, singing songs of love to Sophroniscus and dancing with him in my arms. I wove oak leaves into a crown for him to wear on his head and worshipped him as if he were truly the son of Zeus himself.

"Will you grow to be a sculptor like the grandfather whose name you carry?" I asked my child. He puckered his lips and cooed harmoniously. "Oh, I see!" I exclaimed. "You will grow to be a poet like Alcaeus. Or perhaps a statesman like your great-grandfather Aristides the Just? Surely you will be a lover of wisdom like your father."

I prattled on about everything and nothing. I told him the stories of the gods and goddesses. I pointed out Apollo's chariot in the afternoon sky and told of his twin sister Artemis who guided us safely through childbirth and delivered my beautiful boy. I sang Homer's stories of Hercules, Achilles and Odysseus and Sophocles' stories of Oedipus and Antigone. I recounted every one of Aesop's fables and made up a few of my own. Regardless of my words, my voice magically held Sophroniscus spellbound.

Some days a never-ending fountain of thoughts and ideas flowed through me. Other days I found comfort in the silence as I watched my baby sleep. The wonder of his life became entwined with the wonder of my own ability to conceive, bear and sustain him. Every effort to satisfy his needs seemed to satisfy my own as well.

I found little time to read, but much time for reflection on all that I had read with Lamprocles and discussed with Socrates. Occasionally, I would walk a ways with them in the morning with Sophroniscus cradled to my chest in his sling. Other times we would meet them on their journey home in the evening. Lamprocles was intentionally seeking out doctors from the Koan School of Medicine who lectured at the gymnasium and discussing the merits of midwifery with them. He was more than happy to recount those discussions during our walks and during the evening meal.

I didn't exactly forget about the ominous favor I owed to Xanthippe; it just became further removed from my mind until I no longer gave it a thought. I watched the rising and setting points of the sun creeping north on the horizon until we reached the summer solstice. After remaining in the same place for several days, the sun's comings and goings began to drift south. Once it became apparent that the days were again growing shorter, Xanthippe called upon me for her favor.

Leda delivered the message in the cool of the evening, before Socrates and Lamprocles had returned from the Agora. I was sitting in the courtyard nursing Sophroniscus.

"Mrs. Myrto?" Leda's voice sounded muffled.

"Yes, Leda," I answered. "Come have a seat beside me."

Leda hesitated, but finally sat down. She carried a feeling of uneasiness about her, and her eyes remained fixed on Sophroniscus.

"What is it?" I asked. "Are you all right?"

"Oh, yes ma'am." Leda nodded. "It's not me; it's Mrs. Xanthippe."

Sensing my uncertainty, Sophroniscus began to squirm and fuss.

"What about Xanthippe?" I asked, struggling to settle Sophroniscus.

"She said to tell you that the time has come for the favor." Leda's eyes searched mine, offering no hint of what would be required of me."

"What does she want me to do?"

"She didn't say. She just said that you are to meet her on the hillside of Artemis at sunrise tomorrow," said Leda.

"And what about Sophroniscus?" I asked. "Am I to just leave him here with you? How will he eat?"

Leda shook her head. "She said you would bring Sophroniscus, and that I should pack food for two for a midday meal."

I paused. I really did not know what to make of this strange request. I shifted Sophroniscus to my other breast.

"Do you think she means me any harm?" I asked.

Leda shook her head. "You see Xanthippe as the Trojan Horse, her belly filled with warriors just waiting for the opportunity to attack."

Xanthippe did appear to me as a warship, always prepared to do battle. "Isn't she?"

Again Leda shook her head. "Mrs. Xanthippe means no harm to anyone."

My skepticism escaped in the form of a laugh. "Then you tell me, Leda," I asked. "What's inside Xanthippe?"

"Her belly is full of lost souls," Leda explained, "souls who have finally found a safe place where they can be nurtured and grow."

I stood and put Sophroniscus over my shoulder. I patted his back, bouncing him as I paced. "I came to this house a lost soul, and Xanthippe did nothing to nurture or comfort me."

"Mrs. Myrto," Leda responded, "maybe it's not my place to say, but you have always been safe in this house." She moved toward me and put a hand on my shoulder. "And just look at how you've grown. You didn't need Mrs. Xanthippe to nurture you. You've learned how to nurture yourself."

"So what does she want from me, Leda?" I cried, my voice betraying my fear.

"I really don't know," replied Leda, and I believed her. "But there is one more thing. She said that you are not to say a word to Socrates or Lamprocles, at least not yet. You are to rise as usual, and after they have left for the Agora, go directly to the hill. She will be waiting there for you."

I took a deep breath, followed by another. *What am I afraid of? What can she really do to me? I promised a favor in return for her favor. This promise I shall keep.*

I lay awake in bed most of the night imagining what Xanthippe might have in mind. Was she expecting another baby girl? Did she want me to act as a wet nurse? I looked at Sophroniscus sleeping peacefully between Socrates and me. Could I make enough milk to satisfy another baby?

I must have slipped into a fitful sleep, for suddenly I was dreaming. *I am making my way up the hill. The baby boy I am carrying is not my Sophroniscus. He is hungry and crying. I try to feed him, but I have no milk. I barely have breasts. I am a young girl again. I am taking the baby up to Artemis so that she can care for him.*

As we reach the top of the hill, the baby stops crying. I am happy that the baby is peaceful. But something is wrong. He's not breathing. I reach my finger into his mouth to clear it and find an obol tucked under his tongue. I cry out to Artemis to save us both. "Myrto," a voice calls. It is the voice of my mother. When I try to answer her call, I feel a coin under my tongue as well. I, too, am prepared to pay the ferryman to deliver me into the underworld of Hades to join my mother.

I awakened with a start. Sophroniscus stirred and Socrates rolled over to face us both. "Is everything all right?" he whispered.

I kiss the top of Sophroniscus' head before kissing my husband's lips. "Yes," I murmured.

Socrates drew us both in closer to himself. A moment later I heard him softly snoring. I was not in the habit of keeping secrets from my husband. And I did not share in Leda's trust of Xanthippe's intentions.

22

SOCRATES AND LAMPROCLES rose early and were on their way to the city before sunrise. As soon as they left, Leda brought me breakfast and a satchel packed with a midday meal.

"Has Xanthippe already gone?" I asked.

Leda nodded. "She was gone even before the men stirred."

Leda helped me to tie my pouch around my neck and placed Sophroniscus over my right hip. His neck had grown strong, and he preferred to hold it erect as we walked so that he could see everything going on around him.

I held a strange energy in my heart as we began our journey to the hill of Artemis. Part of me felt surprisingly safe and calm, ready to face my fear and be done with this, come what may. At the same time, a sense of expectancy also stirred within me.

I walked with Sophroniscus past fields of wheat, some awaiting harvest and some already harvested. Even those lying barren from the hot, dry summer rejoiced in the cool morning breeze and the knowledge that the rains would soon come again, making them fertile once more.

I ascended the hill briskly, singing a hymn to Artemis. Sophroniscus clucked along with me, enjoying the song and our pace.

Oh, chariot of Artemis
Harnessed to golden deer
Carry this goddess to waters sweet
And dress her with raiment fair
For she has hunted through the night
Rejoicing in the chase
Arrows launched from bow pulled tight
Have found their lofty place.

Sophroniscus and I traipsed through the dense forest up the hillside like two soldiers marching into battle. As we neared the clearing at the top, our tempo slowed to a silent stop. For a brief moment, I thought I could hear the waves crashing on the not-so-distant rocky shores. The sun's light crept through the surrounding trees, but only a crescent moon appeared dimly overhead.

"Here!" Xanthippe called from off to one side.

As I turned to face her, I noticed she held something in her right hand. She began walking toward us, waving the rectangular object that I still could not recognize. I was surprised to see Korinna following along behind her.

"Good morning." I greeted them both with a confidence I did not quite feel.

Xanthippe wasted no time on salutations or pleasantries. "Korinna has spent the night on this hill and sacrificed her toys to Artemis. She is no longer a child."

Korinna stood tall beside Xanthippe, and I could indeed see that she was not the same child that had welcomed me so many moons ago. *A lifetime ago.* I held Sophroniscus close and waited.

Xanthippe held the object out before me, and I could see that it was a wax-covered writing tablet. "You will teach Korinna to read and write," Xanthippe commanded.

I nodded, taking the tablet in hand, its familiarity bringing me great comfort.

"You will say nothing to anyone about what you are doing until the day that you have completed this task."

Again, I nodded.

"If you are unsuccessful, you will tell no one, and you will still owe me a favor." Xanthippe shifted her eyes from me to Korinna. "If you are successful, you may tell whomever you wish, and you will have fulfilled your promise of a favor to me."

Xanthippe did not wait for my response. She walked hurriedly past and left me standing there staring at Korinna, who appeared more than a bit bewildered.

I turned around and called out, "Xanthippe!" She stopped without turning around. "Must we study only here on the mountain or may we seek out other secluded places as well?"

"Do what you will," she said. "Just make sure that nobody sees you or knows about this." And with that she disappeared into a grove of fir trees.

"Will you really teach me to read and write?" Korinna asked.

"Of course, I will," I replied. "It will be great fun for both of us."

"But what if I fail to learn?" Korinna's voice faltered.

I took her hand, and we began to walk down the hill together. "I cannot promise what you will or will not learn," I told her. "But as long as you desire to learn, I can promise you that you will learn something."

"You don't mind teaching me?" asked Korinna.

"I will be learning right along with you," I replied. "Let's walk down to the sea." I began to teach her the names and sounds of each letter as we walked.

Some days we found a shady place by the river, other days we found a grassy meadow where Sophroniscus could crawl around and explore. As the rains came, we often studied by firelight in a nearby cave or abandoned silver mine. On those days, Sophroniscus would stay behind with Leda and the other girls. He was able to eat soft bread soaked in olive oil and mashed fruits and vegetables by then, and only nursed in the morning and at night.

Socrates and Lamprocles knew that I was up to something. Socrates accepted my promise to tell him when I could, but Lamprocles persisted in cross-examining me on my evasive replies.

"Honestly, Lamprocles," I insisted. "I want to tell you, but I cannot. Not yet."

"But why not?" Lamprocles persevered. His body had grown stronger and his beard much fuller over the past year.

"I just can't. Not now. But soon."

"Promise?" he asked.

"I promise," I said.

Korinna worked diligently to master the letters and their sounds. Her fingers were nimble from years of weaving, and she quickly learned to write as well. We read Hesiod and Heraclitus, just as Lamprocles and I had, but Korinna seemed less inclined to ask questions. She simply read the words before her and awaited my approval.

As her reading skills became stronger we began to study the midwifery book together. This completely captured Korinna's attention as she began applying what she read to her own changing body. After nearly every sentence, she would stop to discuss what exactly the words meant and ask questions about my own experience in marrying Socrates and giving birth to Sophroniscus. My own understanding increased greatly as we studied and discussed the text from both sides of childbirth.

"Someday, when I have a child, will you be there with me?" Korinna asked.

"Of course," I replied. "I will be there for you just like Mama Leda was there for me."

The idea seemed to comfort her and somehow reassured me as well. I wondered how my life might have been different if my mother had taught me to read and studied with me, sharing her wisdom and experience. Of course, in addition to dying, my mother couldn't read. *Thank you, Athena and Hestia, for directing my path to Socrates. Imagine if I had been given instead to my uncle in marriage. Whatever would have become of me?*

As much as I enjoyed spending each day with Korinna, once we had completed the midwifery book, I knew the time had come to report back to Xanthippe.

"Write all of the letters," Xanthippe instructed Korinna. Korinna wrote each letter on the tablet and named each one with confidence and grace.

"Write my name," Xanthippe said. Korinna complied.

"Write this sentence," Xanthippe whispered the words in Korinna's ear. Korinna wrote them with ease. Xanthippe inspected the writing and then handed it to me. "What does it say?" she demanded.

I read the sentence. "Penelope weaves all day while Odysseus is away."

Finally, Xanthippe handed Korinna a piece of parchment I'd never seen before and asked her to read it aloud. Korinna did, and at last Xanthippe appeared satisfied. She turned to me, "You have done well." Then she turned back to Korinna. "Can you teach Iris to read and write?"

Korinna looked at me and smiled. I nodded. "Yes, I can," Korinna replied. "When do we begin?"

It appeared that Xanthippe's intention was for all of the girls to learn to read. This surprised me given Xanthippe herself could not read and did not seem interested in learning. As I pondered what it might be like for every young girl in our household to read, I began to see my own desire to read as the catalyst. I remembered how I felt on that first day in the Agora when Plato had assumed I could read. *What would the world be like if women everywhere could read? How many more books would there be like those written by Theano?*

23

I WAS RELIEVED to finally share my secret work with Socrates and Lamprocles. Even more pleasing was the freedom I now felt to move about the house, whenever I wished, wherever I wished. I would often join the girls in weaving and washing. As we worked together we talked about books and stories and festivals. Xanthippe neither avoided me nor sought me out, but occasionally I would catch her nodding her head approvingly as the girls and I worked together.

On warm and sunny days, Sophroniscus and I would accompany Korinna and Iris to the river or meadow. As they read together, I gathered myrtle blossoms, twigs and leaves that I distilled into oils to add to our soap. Other times I made flower water by boiling what I'd collected in fresh rainwater. I spent more time at home, but less time in our bedroom. I even began taking my meals with Xanthippe, Socrates and Lamprocles. The conversations were often quite lively, although Xanthippe and I still did not address each other directly. We celebrated every festival vicariously through Lamprocles' retelling.

One evening he returned home particularly exuberant. "Myrto," he called, "come see what I have here!" He pulled a papyrus roll from his satchel and handed it to me. The writing was difficult to read at first. The continuous stream of letters seemed unlike the other books that I'd read, and there were blank lines scattered throughout the work. As I studied the text further, I deciphered the names Antigone and Creon and realized that each blank line indicated the beginning of a new scene.

"Oh, Lamprocles!" I cried out. "Can this be the script of Sophocles' play *Antigone?*"

Lamprocles laughed mischievously. "It can be, and it is!" He reached again in his satchel and pulled out another roll. "And now look at this one."

This time my eyes fixed immediately on the infamous names of Oedipus and Jocasta. *"Oedipus the King!"* I clamored.

"Written by Sophocles' own hand," said Lamprocles with a nod.

"Where did you get these?" I asked.

"Sophocles' grandson loaned them to Father," replied Lamprocles.

Socrates put his arm around me and gave me a kiss before taking a seat on the sofa. "I thought you both might enjoy reading them."

I giggled with delight, and then wondered aloud, "How old do you suppose these manuscripts are?"

Lamprocles shrugged, and we both looked to Socrates who was watching us as if we were actors in a comedy.

Socrates cleared his throat and motioned to Lamprocles to pour him a glass of wine. "As you know, even though the chronology of the stories puts *Oedipus the King* before the story of his daughter Antigone, Sophocles produced *Antigone* first and *Oedipus* over a decade later."

As Socrates spoke, Lamprocles poured wine for all of us. "Yes, but how long ago, Father?" Lamprocles asked as he handed a glass to Socrates.

Socrates drank most of the pour and gave a long sigh. "I was probably close to thirty years old when Sophocles entered *Antigone* in the tragedy contest at the festival of Dionysus." Socrates finished the wine in his glass. "Funny thing, though; he didn't win the contest that year."

"What tragic play could be better than *Antigone?*" I asked in disbelief.

Socrates shook his head. "I cannot recall the play that actually won that year."

"Probably something from Aeschylus or Euripides," Lamprocles suggested as he poured more wine for Socrates.

"Not Aeschylus," replied Socrates. "He was dead by then. Must have been Euripides. Yes, I'm quite certain Euripides won it that year."

I was calculating the years in my head. If Socrates was thirty when he saw *Antigone* and in his early forties when Sophocles produced *Oedipus the King,* then even the newer one must be approaching thirty years old.

"How odd that Sophocles never wrote a third play to go with them like most writers of tragedy do," I commented.

Socrates eyes sparkled. "And why do you think that Sophocles never completed the trilogy?"

I looked from Socrates to Lamprocles who could not hide a grin. "I've never heard of a third play," I stammered. "And Sophocles died several years ago."

"All true," Lamprocles interjected. "But now for the most amazing news of all: Before Sophocles died, he did write a play called *Oedipus at Colonus*, and his grandson will be producing it for this year's festival!"

"At Colonus? A play about the events that occurred after *Oedipus the King* and before *Antigone?*" I asked.

Socrates nodded. "How very appropriate that Sophocles ended in the middle, don't you agree?"

I didn't know what to think about the order of the plays, but the desire to attend the production overwhelmed me. I had never known any women to go to the theatre. I did not even consider attending last year with my large, pregnant belly. I walked over to Socrates and placed my hand on his shoulder. "Do you suppose I could go with you to watch the play?"

"Of course you can come, can't she Father!" exclaimed Lamprocles.

"I don't see why not," agreed Socrates. He patted my hand reassuringly. "There are often foreign women scattered around the edges of the crowd, so you would not be the only woman present." Socrates pulled me around and seated me across his lap so that I could face him. "I would be most pleased to have you in the seat on my right and Lamprocles seated to my left."

"Then it's settled!" proclaimed Lamprocles. "Myrto and I will study *Oedipus the King* and *Antigone* together just like old times, and then we can all attend *Oedipus at Colonus* next month."

Socrates assured me that Sophroniscus would be fine with Leda and the girls looking after him, so the next morning I once again accompanied Socrates and Lamprocles to the Agora. When we arrived, Plato was there under the laurel tree waiting for Socrates. From the look on his face, I knew he was surprised to see me, but he appeared pleased nevertheless.

"Good morning, Socrates," he said, shaking Socrates hand. Lamprocles also received a greeting and handshake.

"Good morning, Plato," I said, extending my hand as well.

Plato reached out as if to shake my hand, but then swiftly lifted my hand to his lips, bestowing a kiss upon it. His lips felt soft and warm against the back of my hand. "Good morning, Myrto," he said with a smile. I wished that I could tell him how his belief that I could read had led to all of the young girls in our home learning to read. But the words did not come.

"What's that you've got around your neck?" asked Lamprocles.

Plato removed the thickly woven cord from around his neck and held up a beautifully decorated wineskin for us to see. "Do you like it?" he asked. "I won it last week in a drinking contest at the Festival of Flowers."

He handed it first to Lamprocles, who looked at it only briefly before passing it to me.

"See the ram with golden horns?" Plato asked, moving closer to me, placing his hands over mine on the wineskin and turning it to display the ornamentation. He followed the swirl of the horns with his finger. "That's all real gold," he said. Then he took the wineskin from me and handed it to Socrates. "Please, Socrates, accept this gift from your humble student."

As Socrates thanked him, Lamprocles and I excused ourselves and went to find a place to study the plays of Sophocles.

"Shall we go back to the Graces?" asked Lamprocles.

I nodded. "That would be fine."

We took turns reading, arguing over which three characters were on stage at any given time and who was saying what. Although I enjoyed this immensely, the city did not seem to energize me as it had when we first began studying here. My mind frequently returned to Sophroniscus, wondering if he was playing happily or needing comfort.

"What's wrong?" Lamprocles asked, interrupting my thoughts of home.

"Nothing," I said. "I was just thinking that maybe tomorrow we could study in the meadow or near the river. Would you mind?"

"I don't care where we read," replied Lamprocles. "I just want you to pay attention to what we're reading."

"Then perhaps Sophroniscus could come with us. We could bring along one of the girls to watch him," I suggested.

Lamprocles studied me from my head to my feet. "You know, Myrto, you've changed."

I laughed. "Me?" I said. "What about you? Your voice has dropped an octave and your beard is as full as any soldier's."

He stroked his shiny, black beard. "It is getting full, isn't it? And look at this." He flexed his arms. I watched in amazement how the muscles bulged on command.

"All of that time at the gymnasium has paid off," I said, happy to give him a compliment.

"I do enjoy exercising, but I'd still rather read and talk with you." He leaned back against a stone and put his hands behind his head, continuing to flex his biceps beyond what it took to support his head. "Do you know what I really wish, Myrto?" He sat up and looked at me in earnest. "I wish we could find another book like that midwifery book to read together."

For the first time in nearly two years, my mind flashed back to a book Socrates had shown me before any of the markings could speak to me—the book written by the same hand as the midwifery book. I nodded. "I know what we can read after the festival of Dionysus."

24

THE NEXT MORNING Leda sent us off with enough food to feed a small army, which is what we had become by the time we left the house. When Korinna heard that Lamprocles and I would be studying by the River Illisus, she asked if she and Iris might join us in our studies. Leda suggested that Myrrine come, too, to care for Sophroniscus while the rest of us read the plays of Sophocles. Myrrine was about six months younger than Iris, and everyone expected that Iris would soon be teaching her to read and write as well.

"What horrible fate," Lamprocles reflected on the tragedy as we walked. "I can think of nothing more heinous than murdering your father and marrying your mother."

"I agree," I said, "but it seems Oedipus might have avoided this if he had simply followed the Delphic Oracle's instruction to each of us: 'Know Thyself.'"

"Are you saying that Oedipus brought all of this upon himself?" Lamprocles asked in a reproaching tone. "He did not bring the prophecy upon himself. He was doomed before his true parents conceived him. How could he know that he had been abandoned by the king and queen of Thebes at birth, rescued by a shepherd, and raised by the king and queen of Corinth?"

"But when he learned of the prophecy, he chose to flee Corinth. If he'd only talked to his parents there about it, they would have told him that he was not their natural son. By running away, he brought everything he feared upon himself," I insisted.

Day after day during our reading we talked about fate and the choices we make. As we finished *Oedipus the King,* I remained firmly convinced that when we try too hard to avoid a fate we bring it upon ourselves and, likewise, when we seek to judge others, we unwittingly judge ourselves. Lamprocles appeared less convinced than I.

As we read *Antigone,* we decided it might be entertaining to act out the play. Of course, in the original production all of the characters were played by men. Lamprocles decided that he should be Antigone, and that I should be Creon.

"But Antigone is a woman and Creon is a man," I objected. "Wouldn't it make more sense for you to be Creon and for me to be Antigone?"

"But Antigone is the main character, and I want to be the main character," Lamprocles responded.

"Creon is the main character," I insisted. "He's the reason Antigone and Creon's wife Eurydice and their son Haemon all kill themselves. He's the only one left living at the end."

"You just don't want to be Creon because you don't like him," said Lamprocles.

"No," I said. "You're the one who doesn't like Creon, and that's why you want to be Antigone."

"Yes," admitted Lamprocles. "So you get to be Creon."

"Fine," I conceded, "but let's have Korinna be Antigone and you can be all of the other parts."

We asked Korinna to be our third actor, and Iris, Myrrine and Sophroniscus became our chorus. Our chorus required a substantial amount of assistance from our main actors. Sophroniscus did prove to be a good little wailer every time someone died. Lamprocles played the role of Creon's son Haemon with great passion, both in defense of his betrothed Antigone and in attempting to persuade Creon that the gods would punish him for ordering that Antigone be locked in a cave to die. Though it wasn't really supposed to be acted out on stage, Lamprocles and Korinna portrayed both the ardor and the deaths of the ill-fated lovers with such fervor that for a moment I would have believed that the two of them had truly fallen in love.

Creon didn't appear to feel much remorse for the death of Antigone, but I could feel tears stinging my eyes as I delivered Creon's final lines:

"Lead me away! I am the rash man who killed you, my son, and you too, my wife. Alas, wretch that I am, I cannot look on either of you; I have nothing to hold onto. Everything these hands have touched has turned to grief and fate has come down upon my head."

I felt genuine sympathy for the man who finally understood that he had brought this sorrow upon himself through his own foolish pride.

By the time the festival of Dionysus arrived, Lamprocles had decided that Korinna should accompany us to see *Oedipus at Colonus.* Thousands upon thousands of people poured into the theatre, a semicircular arena built into a natural hollow of the hillside in the Acropolis. From the top of the grassy slopes we could look out over the stage and catch a glimpse of the Aegean Sea. Men dressed as billy goats had already moved the large wooden statue of Dionysus from the temple to the place in the theatre where it would remain throughout the festival.

Wine flowed freely and the aroma of freshly charred beef lingered in the air. Our bellies were full of meat from the cattle sacrificed in honor of Dionysus. Socrates led us down into the very middle of the theatre where we found room for the four of us to sit on one of the wooden planks. Lamprocles insisted that Korinna and I sit together in the middle with Socrates on my left and Lamprocles on her right. The crowd buzzed with excitement until the drone of a double-piped aulos settled like a cloud upon us.

Two actors, one wearing the mask of Oedipus and one wearing the mask of Antigone took the stage. Their bodies, clad in long, brightly colored costumes, moved slowly and with great precision. When the chorus finally entered, the fifteen men resembled a single giant octopus with many heads and arms, all moving simultaneously, but with rather awkward coordination.

Korinna gripped my hand as the chorus chanted for Oedipus and Antigone not to enter the sacred grove outside Colonus: *"Turn around! Come back! You have gone too far!"*

During one of Oedipus' elaborate apologies for his atrocious crimes and exile from Thebes, Socrates slipped his arm around my waist and drew me closer to him. I studied my husband for a moment before returning my attention to the stage. Sitting there with Socrates, I began to see Oedipus in a new light. In the end Oedipus always defended his own actions as honorably intended, claiming he killed his father in self-defense and blaming the city of Thebes for offering his mother to him as a wife.

The chorus wailed, bemoaning life and glorifying death, *"Not to be born is the condition that surpasses all others. But once man is born, the next best thing is to return with utmost haste to where he has come from."*

Indeed, I had the sense that if Oedipus somehow had it all to do over again, he would do nothing differently. Even as death drew near, Oedipus blessed his daughters for standing by him and cursed his sons for banishing him to a strange land. Both his blessings and his curses brought suffering and death.

The crowd around us seemed drawn together in the fear of impending doom, yet I felt strangely separate. Korinna and Lamprocles appeared completely mesmerized. When I turned to Socrates, he smiled. "It's a tragedy, you know," he whispered in my ear.

I nodded. "Haven't we all suffered enough tragedy in our own lives?"

"Suffering naturally seeks companionship," he whispered back.

"I find the whole elaborate production much more troubling than natural," I confessed.

"Perhaps you would better enjoy a comedy," replied Socrates. "It's the same collective foolishness, but without the pretense of public virtue."

I shook my head. "I think I prefer reading books."

Socrates nodded. "Reading is good. Especially when it leads to contemplation and dialogue."

As we journeyed home that evening, Socrates and I walked behind Lamprocles and Korinna listening to them discuss the lives of Oedipus, Antigone and Creon. They extolled Antigone's devotion to her family and her respect for the gods. They decried Creon's stubbornness and shortsightedness. They remained quite baffled by Oedipus and his fate, well-persuaded that he suffered his deeds more than he committed them.

25

AFTER THE FESTIVAL of Dionysus, Lamprocles and I began studying the other book of Theano entitled *The One*. Her words spoke
directly to my soul inspiring the purest sense of awe I had ever experienced. She wrote that the genesis of all life, light and dark, male
and female, is one. There is only one and the perceived absence of
one, which is an openness full of potential also known as nothing.
The energy of life pulsates like our own heartbeat. The one contracts, then opens to refill, contracts, and opens again.

All that ever was, all that is now and all that there ever will be
exists within the pulsating energy: O1O1O1O1O1. The one encompasses all being, and the openness encompasses all potential
for becoming. As Lamprocles read, I placed my hands over my
heart and closed my eyes, feeling my own heartbeat. My ears filled
with the dark mystery of rushing blood, and my eyes beheld a new
inner light. I felt the breath of the universe within me.

Theano told of those who traveled far to the East and returned
with an image of the one as a circle and the source of becoming
within. This powerful symbol of light and darkness, male and female, being and becoming appears as a circle with a river winding
through the center. On each side of the river exists a single large
droplet of water, one white and one black. In the center of the

white droplet is planted the seed of darkness, and in the center of the black droplet is planted the seed of light.

The travelers demonstrated for Theano and other Pythagoreans the dance of the sun's light and the earth's shadow that created this image. They erected a pole measuring slightly less than two and one-half meters perpendicular to the earth's surface and recorded the shadow images over the course of a year. The shortest shadow occurred on summer solstice and formed the tip of the black droplet and the source of the river dividing the droplets. The longest shadow occurred on winter solstice and formed the tip of the white droplet and the mouth of the river flowing into the surrounding circle.

The travelers called the darkness yin and the light yang. Yin is born at summer solstice, and yang is born at winter solstice. Together yin and yang represent the unity and equality of light and darkness, male and female, coexisting in balance and harmony. This is the order and pattern of the universe, the path to prosperity and flourishing. Neither yin nor yang is superior; neither exists apart from the other. Any attempt at hierarchy or domination disrupts the natural flow creating disaster and destruction.

"Lamprocles," I asked, "do you suppose that it is the domination of men that has caused continuous war and the plague?"

Lamprocles shook his head. "It does not stand to reason," he replied. "States go to war over land and resources."

"Or a woman, such as Helen of Troy," I added.

"Yes," said Lamprocles, "but recall that the Amazon women also fought in the Trojan War."

"A nation of women warriors is still a nation without balance between men and women," I replied. "Do you suppose that there exists anywhere a state where men and women live together in perfect balance?"

"Maybe that is what the Pythagoreans intend," said Lamprocles. "Still, their society is so secretive and mysterious that it is hard to say."

"This book we're reading does not feel like the words of a man or the words of a woman," I told him. "It feels like a greater truth. It feels like wisdom."

"I don't know," Lamprocles said. "It's just so different than the mathematical calculations and geometrical proofs that I've always associated with Pythagoras."

"It's also quite different from the hygiene and medicine we studied in the midwifery book," I agreed. "Does the fact that this is different make it untrue?" I asked.

"I don't know if it's true or not, because I don't know how to test it," said Lamprocles. "I can work the mathematical calculations myself, and we were able to follow the instructions and advice of the midwifery book when Sophroniscus was born. I just don't know what to do with this or where to start."

"We could erect a pole and record the shadows and see if we find the same image of yin and yang described by the travelers," I offered.

Lamprocles studied a sketch of the shadow images in the book. "The pattern of shadows around the pole makes sense. And the swirling line dividing the light from the shadow appears very natural to me—similar to the swirl in a seashell or a ram's horn." Lamprocles picked up a stick and drew a circle in the dirt. He drew a series of O's and 1's; then he started drawing yin and yang within each open circle.

"It's like the river of Heraclitus surrounded by the being of Parmenides," I said. "Together they are the genesis."

Lamprocles dropped the stick and stared at his scratchings in the earth. After a long while he looked at me, eyes full of wonder. "It is, isn't it?" he pondered. "Still, if I spend a year recording the shadows and produce the same image, how does that make the rest of it true?"

"And even if your recordings produce a different image, would that destroy the underlying principles represented by the symbol?" I asked.

Lamprocles sighed. "If it's true, it's true regardless of whether I can prove it."

"And if it's not true?" I asked.

"Then it's even harder to prove a negative," Lamprocles responded. He began to brush away the images he'd drawn in the dirt.

"Does it really matter whether or not you can prove it if you believe in your heart that it's true?" I asked.

"The only way to persuade others is by proof," he insisted.

"But I believe it, even without your proof," I said. I carefully rolled up the papyrus and placed it securely in Lamprocles' satchel.

Lamprocles brushed the dust from his tunic and stood. "Why?" he asked. "Why do you believe it?"

The way he stood over me suddenly made me feel inferior. I rose to my feet to look him squarely in the face. I realized for the first time that he was actually quite a bit taller than I these days. Still, standing on my own two feet before him, I felt every bit his equal. In many ways we were different as night and day, but no different in human value.

"I believe it because it feels true to me," I said simply.

"But how can you persuade someone else that you are right and he is wrong?" asked Lamprocles.

"I do not wish to persuade anyone of anything," I said. I handed Lamprocles his satchel.

"Well, I do!" exclaimed Lamprocles. He slung the satchel over his shoulder and put his hands on his hips. "What's the point of being right if you can't prove it?"

"Maybe the point isn't about who is right and who is wrong," I suggested. "Maybe the point is that today I feel a deeper sense of truth than I did yesterday. As I continue to think and grow, my understanding will continue to change as well. Maybe it's more about seeking wisdom than being right."

Lamprocles threw up his hands in exasperation. "Every time I think I'm really getting it, you say something like that and all of my thoughts just go up in flames!"

I smiled and nodded. "And every time I think I am beginning to really know something, I am reminded that someone older and wiser and much more experienced than I understands that he knows nothing."

"Right," Lamprocles sighed. "What do I know?"

26

THAT EVENING AS we ate, Lamprocles and I discussed our reading with Socrates.

"The symbol of the yin and the yang intrigues me," said Socrates. "In fact, it reminds me of a book by Democritus called *Little Cosmology.*" He broke off a large piece of bread and passed it to Lamprocles.

"I've heard of Democritus, but I didn't think anyone took him seriously," replied Lamprocles. He also tore a chunk of bread from the loaf and placed it in a small dish of olive oil. "Even Plato said that the papyrus he writes upon is more valuable for burning than for reading." He passed the bread to Xanthippe, who kept the greater share and placed the remaining portion between us.

"Perhaps," replied Socrates, "but Democritus attempted to resolve Parmenides' being and Heraclitus' becoming by conceiving of an eternal, indivisible particle called the atom." Socrates poured some wine in a bowl for me and filled both of our glasses before passing the jar to Lamprocles.

"What exactly is an atom?" I asked as I broke my bread into small pieces and dropped them into the bowl of wine to soften.

"According to Democritus, it's exactly what its name suggests: something that is 'uncuttable.' Atoms are like little, eternal, unchanging beings that combine to form larger, visible objects," explained Socrates.

"But what happens when the object ceases to exist?" Lamprocles asked.

"The atoms disperse," replied Socrates. "They simply move on to combine with other atoms and form other objects."

"What about fire?" I asked. "Can fire destroy atoms?"

"Not according to Democritus," said Socrates.

I held up a piece of softened bread. "So this wine and this bread are both made of atoms?"

Socrates nodded. "If Democritus is to be believed, they are indeed."

"So the wine begins to disperse the bread atoms and wine atoms by mixing them together," Lamprocles hypothesized. "Then Myrto uses her teeth to chew the bread into even smaller pieces, mixing them with saliva and swallowing them where the juices in the stomach break them down even further?"

"And inside my body, some atoms join with my blood and circulate through my body providing nourishment, while others pass through as waste?" I asked.

"Waste!" Xanthippe grunted. "If you don't mind, I'd like to eat my meal without analyzing the holy crap out of it!"

Socrates and Lamprocles both laughed. I remained silent, consumed by the enigma of atoms and immune to Xanthippe's cutting remarks.

"What about wind and water?" asked Lamprocles. "Can they be made of atoms, too?"

"They must be," said Socrates, "or Democritus is greatly mistaken."

This puzzled me. "If an atom cannot be divided, and atoms make up everything, then how can they move about and change form?" I asked. "They must either pass through each other or there must somehow be room for them to move."

"Good point," said Socrates. "What do you think Lamprocles?"

Lamprocles contemplated this for some time. Finally, he replied, "In *The One,* Theano suggests that all is one, but that the one is actually a pulsating series of nothing and something."

"Excellent connection," Socrates said, nodding his approval. "What Myrto has called 'room to move,' Democritus would call 'space' or 'the void.'"

"A universe of something and nothing," I whispered.

"Where nothing always has the potential to become something," Lamprocles reflected. "Anything really."

Socrates looked at me and smiled. I nodded. "And the only constant is the change from something to nothing back to something and again into nothing." I concluded.

"So if an atom were large enough to observe with the human eye, would it look like the yin-yang image?" Lamprocles asked.

"What is this yin-yang image you keep talking about?" Xanthippe interrupted.

"Let me show you, Mother." Lamprocles jumped to his feet and returned with a tablet. He swiftly drew a circle. "It is a circle divided by a winding river, like this." He drew the twisting line and began shading one side. "And half is light, and the other half is shadow, like this." He explained briefly about erecting the pole and recording the shadows for an entire year.

"And you think that every one of us and everything in this room is nothing but a bunch of those little circles?" Xanthippe cackled. "All of this reading has finally driven you mad!" She banged the table with her fist before taking up her bread and continuing to eat.

"I don't know whether it's true or not, Mother," replied Lamprocles. "We're just thinking about it and testing whether or not it could be true."

"Democritus never really decided on a shape for the atom," Socrates added. He combed through his beard with his fingers to remove the bread crumbs and pursed his thick lips. "He originally postulated a triangle, but then decided that perhaps atoms were all different shapes."

"Well, if you take away the actual circle," said Lamprocles, "you're left with three parts: the river that runs through the center, light and darkness."

I stared at the table top. "An infinite number of centers, surrounded by light and dark, but no circumference anywhere?" I felt a flash of insight, but it almost seemed too simple. And neither Socrates nor Lamprocles responded to my inquiry.

"Where can we get this book, *Little Cosmology?*" Lamprocles asked. "I've never seen it in the Agora."

"Plato has more books than anyone, but I think Lamprocles is correct that Plato has no appreciation at all for Democritus," Socrates replied. "The only person I would know to ask would be Aspasia."

"Your former teacher?" I asked.

Socrates nodded. "She may have kept all of Pericles' books and papers."

Lamprocles' face brightened. "Will you ask her?" Lamprocles beseeched him.

Socrates clapped his hands together and then raised them up and out toward us. "I think we should all go ask her," he said, his voice full of adventure.

I wasn't sure who "all" included. I sneaked a peak at Xanthippe, and she appeared uncertain, too. *Does Xanthippe want to join us? It is one thing for me to sit at her table, in her house, in the world that she controls. It is quite another for her to venture out into a world she neither knows nor controls.* My heart quickened as I reminded myself that while I may still be afraid of Xanthippe, perhaps she is also afraid of me.

I took a deep breath, turned to Xanthippe and addressed her directly for the first time since I had asked if Leda could assist with Sophroniscus' birth. "Would you like to join us?" I asked. I placed my hands in my lap so that no one could see them shaking.

She stared at me in silence. Lamprocles' eyes betrayed his astonishment, but Socrates only smiled.

"If you wish to walk with Lamprocles and Socrates, I will follow with Sophroniscus," I offered, making it clear that I intended to show her every respect outside of this home as I had within it.

"I've never met Aspasia," Xanthippe replied, looking at Lamprocles first and then at Socrates. "I believe I would like to go."

"Excellent, my dear," replied Socrates. I wasn't sure if he was talking to me or to Xanthippe, but somehow it didn't matter. "Tomorrow we journey together to the house of Aspasia."

27

WE LEFT AT sunrise and spent most of the morning walking to the house of Aspasia. She lived on the opposite side of the city on the sheep farm owned by her second husband Lysicles. As we walked, I wondered how any woman once married to a man as rich and powerful as Pericles could take a second husband. Of course, General Lysicles had died some years ago, too.

Lamprocles frequently walked beside me rather than ahead of me with his parents, and carried Sophroniscus most of the way. Sophroniscus was well past being tightly wrapped to my body in a tunic. At times he walked, but his interest lay in the world around us rather than in our destination. Lamprocles and I each took a hand so that he could lift his little legs and swing or take Herculean jumps in the direction we wanted him to go. Lamprocles entertained us both with tales of Odysseus' adventures following the Trojan War.

As we approached the house of Aspasia, the late morning sun illuminated the face of the elegant mansion as if it were a true temple of Apollo. A sense of quiet excitement and anticipation connected us. Even Sophroniscus blinked quietly with awe. Socrates knocked on the house door igniting the bark of several dogs. After much rattling of bars and bolts, an attendant appeared.

"Socrates!" the man cried with delight. "Aspasia will be so pleased to see you! Do come in!"

Socrates introduced us each in turn so that we might be properly announced to Aspasia. "How is Aspasia?" he asked.

The man shrugged. "Her time with us is nearing its end. Yet the weaker her body grows, the stronger her mind and spirit become." We passed through a long, dark corridor and back into the sunlight of a well-tended court. The man brought us water to drink and to cleanse ourselves of the long walk. "Please make yourselves comfortable while I announce you."

Sophroniscus ran from white violets to blue hyacinths chasing a butterfly. Xanthippe reclined on a couch, surrounded by red and white roses. Her eyes followed Sophroniscus as he danced throughout the courtyard. Not long after we were all refreshed the man returned and ushered us into a dining room with seven ornate couches arranged along the walls, the head of one couch abutting the foot of the next. The doorway was somewhat off-center, creating a natural inclination to move to the right into the openness of the room, but a reclining figure on the second couch to our left captured our attention.

"Aspasia!" cried Socrates, kneeling beside her and showering her with affection.

"Forgive me for not rising to greet you properly," she said, "but I am indeed delighted to see you and your family." Her voice sang the words, creating an enchanting melody. As her deep blue eyes met mine, they drew me into a profoundly calm and safe place. Sophroniscus ran to her side and wriggled his body in between Socrates and the couch.

"May I present my sons, Lamprocles and Sophroniscus," said Socrates, motioning to each in turn. Lamprocles approached and kissed her hand with respect. Sophroniscus just touched her hand and giggled. "And may I also present my wives, Xanthippe and Myrto." We each bowed in turn. Men and women began carrying in trays of food and jars of wine, setting them on the tables in front of the couches.

As Socrates and Aspasia exchanged news of family and mutual friends, one alabaster jar on the table before Aspasia completely mesmerized me. Etched into the side of the jar was a symbol similar to the yin yang, but also different. Instead of the dark seed in the light water droplet and the light seed in the dark water droplet, the seeds were joined in the middle into a concentric circle. The circles were turned so that the river ran through them horizontally, like an ocean wave on the horizon. It looked rather like the sun setting on the ocean.

Once the tables were set, Aspasia bid us all to find a place and begin eating. Socrates took the couch nearest Aspasia and facing her with his feet in the corner of the room behind her head. Lamprocles took the couch next to Socrates, and Xanthippe took the middle couch on the wall opposite Aspasia. Rather than reclining on either side of Xanthippe, Sophroniscus and I shared the couch nearest Aspasia's feet where I could continue to study the alabaster jar.

As we ate, Aspasia talked to Socrates about the mounting suspicion that had followed them both for decades. "Ever since those ridiculous comedies by Aristophanes," said Aspasia. Aristophanes had written a comedy called *The Acharnians* more than 20 years ago that was most unflattering to Aspasia. Not long after that, he also wrote *The Clouds* portraying Socrates as a pompous, air-headed fool.

Socrates nodded and gave a hearty laugh. "It's only because your beauty rivals Helen of Troy that people believed you alone launched our wars with Sparta!"

"You've always flattered me, Socrates," Aspasia said shaking her head. "Still, the image Aristophanes' painted of you as a buffoon in *The Clouds* may bring you harm even now. There are still those who talk of bringing charges against you for impiety."

This was news to me. After the Thirty Tyrants were overthrown, I'd thought Socrates safe again. But I'd spent little time in the Agora since Sophroniscus was born to hear any talk for myself. I glanced at Lamprocles, who seemed to be avoiding my gaze.

"These are the same charges they threatened to bring against you after *The Acharnians* took first place at the Lenaea festival." Socrates laughed. "The older I get, the less I worry about the gossip," he said. "No one has posted a complaint against me yet."

Yet. The word lingered uneasily in my mind. Socrates was approaching 70 years of age and unlikely to survive a prison sentence. I ate my food in silence.

When the meal was finished, Aspasia asked, "So what brings you to visit on this fine day?"

Socrates turned to Lamprocles and nodded. Lamprocles sat up to face Aspasia more directly. "We have read the books by Theano that you've given Socrates and have come in search of another book."

Aspasia nodded. "What is it that you seek?"

"*Little Cosmology* by Democritus," Lamprocles replied.

"I've read it," Aspasia responded. "That and *Big Cosmology* by Democritus' teacher Leucippus, but I cannot say whether or not I still have either one." Aspasia called for an attendant. "Show Lamprocles to my library and give him a small cart that he can fill with whatever books he chooses," she instructed. Then she turned back to Lamprocles. "Whatever books you find that interest you, you are welcome to keep."

As Lamprocles departed, Aspasia motioned to Xanthippe to move to the couch where he had been sitting. "I have something for you, too, Xanthippe," said Aspasia, "but first you must answer three questions. Will you indulge me and answer my questions honestly?"

Xanthippe appeared puzzled, but responded, "I will."

"Very well," sang Aspasia. "If your neighbor had finer gold jewelry than yours, would you prefer your own jewelry or your neighbor's?"

Xanthippe looked to Socrates who nodded his encouragement for her to answer sincerely. Xanthippe studied the rings on her fingers and the bracelets on her wrists. She clasped the necklace in the palms of her hands and took a deep breath.

"I would prefer my neighbor's," she replied. I had the sense that Xanthippe was hoping that Aspasia would send her off with a treasure of gold and jewels. I looked first at Aspasia, then at my own hands. Neither Aspasia nor I wore a single jewel or piece of gold.

"And if your neighbor's clothes were more precious than yours, would you prefer yours or your neighbor's?" asked Aspasia.

This time Xanthippe did not delay. "I would prefer my neighbor's," she confessed.

"And if your neighbor had a better husband than you, would you prefer her husband over your own?"

Xanthippe's face reddened, and she remained silent for quite a long time.

"No man could be better than Socrates." I thought and heard the words simultaneously, and for a moment believed I must have spoken them aloud. But it was Xanthippe, not I, who answered Aspasia's final question.

"You have answered truly, Xanthippe," said Aspasia. She reached behind her and pulled out a stunning woolen tunic, woven from beautifully dyed yarn. As she unfolded the tunic, a necklace dropped into her lap. Aspasia lifted the gold chain with her right hand and held the yellow dangling charm at the end with her other hand for all to see. "An amber horse," she said. "Come closer and accept my gift, Xanthippe."

As Aspasia handed the necklace to Xanthippe, there was a sudden, loud pop. "Oh!" cried Xanthippe.

Aspasia just smiled. "Rub the amber against the wool again," she instructed. Xanthippe complied. "Now hand it back to me." When Xanthippe returned the necklace to her, there was another loud pop. This time I saw a spark fly, too.

"Did you see that?" asked Aspasia. "It's like a little lightning bolt. We each have the power of Zeus within us. You especially, Xanthippe. You are charged with a great energy capable of tearing things down or of building them up. It's your power and your choice."

"And you want me to choose to build things up?" asked Xanthippe.

"On the contrary," replied Aspasia handing the necklace back to Xanthippe. "Sometimes you have to tear things down before you can rebuild. I only want you to remember that you have this power and choose wisely how you will use it."

"I will," replied Xanthippe. "Thank you." She gave Aspasia a hug and once again we heard the loud pop. This time both women laughed together like old friends.

Aspasia took a deep breath. Our visit seemed to be tiring her. Socrates stood to leave. "Shall we let you rest now?" he asked.

"Not yet," said Aspasia. "Why don't you and Xanthippe take Sophroniscus and go find Lamprocles. I wish to speak with Myrto alone."

28

"YOU ARE EVEN more beautiful than they say," Aspasia said once the others had left. I blushed, but I felt more flattered than embarrassed. "Come sit beside me on my couch." I sat at Aspasia's side and let her cradle my hand in hers. Her face bore the deep wrinkles of many years on this earth, but her eyes remained clear and bright. I felt a warm, surge of energy when our eyes met and many moments passed before Aspasia broke the spell of silence.

"You, too, will have choices to make in the coming days," Aspasia told me. "Is there something that you would like to ask me?"

Questions flooded my mind, but I could not find the words to ask what was really on my heart. *Is Socrates in danger? And what will become of me and Sophroniscus if something happens to Socrates? Perhaps it is better not to know the future.* I closed my eyes and breathed deeply, searching for something else to ask instead. Finally, I nodded and opened my eyes.

"I want to know about the symbol on the alabaster jar," I whispered, casting my gaze toward the table.

"Pick it up, and hold it in your hands," instructed Aspasia. I gently lifted the smooth, marbled jar and held it in both hands. "Like alabaster, you are a soft stone Myrto."

The jar felt heavy and cold. As I raised it up to study the carvings, I found it contained olive oil with a rose and cinnamon fragrance. "This symbol," I said. "It looks like the yin-yang that Theano wrote about, yet it is decidedly different."

"Tell me how it is different," said Aspasia.

"It looks like a sunset at sea," I told her.

"If that is a sunset, what is this?" Aspasia asked. She turned the jar around in my hands so that I could see the same symbol carved on the other side, only upside down.

"A sunrise, I suppose."

"Yes," Aspasia agreed. "The only difference between the sunrise and the sunset is your point of view."

"But what does it mean?" I asked, turning the jar around again from sunrise to sunset.

"The symbol represents the human soul, Myrto," said Aspasia. "This world that we live in is a world of shadows. The truth is a world of light. In the center is the mind's eye, connecting body and spirit."

I ran my finger over the dark swirl. "This is my body," I said. Aspasia nodded. "And this is my spirit?" I asked, pointing to the swirl of light. Again Aspasia nodded. "And my mind is both light and dark?"

"Yes," Aspasia replied. "Each of us is born with a mind half-opened. Some of us, like Socrates, spend a lifetime opening the eye as wide as we can. Others seem to lose their curiosity and child-like wonder. With each passing year, the eye closes further."

"But they, too, can open their eyes if they choose, can't they?"

"They live in darkness," Aspasia replied. When they see someone with a light as bright as Socrates, it hurts their eyes. They never give their eyes a chance to adjust."

"What about the gods?" I asked. "Are their eyes always open and able to adjust to light and darkness equally?"

"We are the gods and goddesses, Myrto," said Aspasia. She placed her hands over mine which were still holding the jar. "We have created them in our image because we are afraid to acknowledge our own divinity."

I could feel my hands trembling. "I'm afraid I don't understand," I said. "Surely you don't mean to say that human beings created earth, wind, fire and water?"

"I mean to say that the creator of all is one," said Aspasia. She removed the alabaster jar from my hands and placed it on the table. Then she took both my hands in hers.

"One what?" I asked.

"One Mother-Father Godde," she replied. "A Godde who not only created us, but continues to create through us."

"Oh, Aspasia, please don't talk like this," I pleaded. "Anyone who says such things surely would be charged with impiety. You could be excommunicated from Athens or even put to death for such heresy."

"I'm only telling you what I've come to know." Aspasia reached again for the alabaster jar. "My mind's eye has opened wide. It is time for me to abandon the shadows and return to the light." She held the jar up between us and slowly turned it over, dumping the oil on both of us.

I bowed my head and wept.

Aspasia began rubbing the scented oil into our hands and arms. Before long I also began rubbing the oil into my legs, and then hers. As we massaged away the oil, we massaged away my tears.

"Now that my jar is empty, I give it to you," said Aspasia. She handed me the jar, upside down demonstrating that it was indeed empty. "You may carry the empty jar with you just as it is, or you may right it, and fill it with whatever you choose."

I nodded, taking the jar and cradling it in my arms like an infant.

"And now I have a question for you," said Aspasia. "When were you last visited by the Mene?"

"The Mene?" I asked. I only knew the word as a verb—to remain, to stand fast, to wait at home. "What is the Mene?"

Aspasia laughed, but her laugh was not unkind. "The Mene is a goddess of the months."

When her meaning sank in, I blushed. "It has been two moons since my last blood," I confessed.

"That's what I thought," Aspasia told me.

"How can you tell?" I asked, eager to learn her secret.

"I cannot tell," Aspasia explained. "I just knew. Not only by observing you with an open mind, but also by watching Socrates. He is such the proud father."

"After the baby is born, we will visit you again," I promised.

Aspasia shook her head. "I will not be here, child."

My throat tightened and my eyes filled with tears. A stabbing pain pierced my heart unlike any I'd known since the death of my own mother. "You mean I'll never see you again?"

Aspasia smiled and stroked my cheek. "You will not see my old body with your beautiful brown eyes, but you will feel me and know I am with you. We are one spirit, Myrto."

I hugged her and let her hold me until my body and the jar could not contain all of the love. As I stood to go, Aspasia whispered, "You have a strong spirit and a strong mind, Myrto. You must use your head, but always follow your heart."

29

THE JOURNEY HOME from Aspasia's house passed quickly. Lamprocles and Xanthippe led the way. As they chattered about the wondrous home and library of Aspasia, Sophroniscus slept in Lamprocles' cart surrounded by books. Socrates and I followed in silence. There were no words, no questions and no answers between us. He simply held my hand as we walked together.

That night as the rest of the house slept, I lay awake in Socrates' arms, still pondering Aspasia. Socrates kissed my forehead. Then, as if tasting my thoughts, he asked, "So what did you think of Aspasia."

I kissed his forehead, but learned nothing of his thoughts. I sighed. "I think that we should name our first daughter Aspasia," I said.

Socrates laughed softly. "A lovely idea," he agreed.

That night I dreamed of our beautiful daughter, Aspasia. Her beauty radiated from deep inside her heart and mind. Everything around her danced in friendly harmony with her inner beauty. A simple wisdom adorned her with riches beyond all of the gold and jewels in Athens. I carried this dream in my heart as my baby's body formed in my belly.

I filled my alabaster vase with olive oil. Every day I rubbed the oil into my skin to keep it soft and moist. Every night I rubbed the oil into Socrates' back, shoulders, arms and hands.

That winter felt colder than usual. A voracious appetite for food replaced my insatiable appetite for reading and talking. I found contentment in tending to my growing belly and the growing thoughts in my mind. I stayed inside, weaving and watching the people around me.

Lamprocles had found both *Little Cosmology* by Democritus and *Big Cosmology* by Leucippus in Aspasia's library. He and Korinna studied them together.

"Are you sure you won't join us, Myrto?" Lamprocles asked each morning.

"Not today," I would say. "Maybe tomorrow."

But each day I found that I did not want to focus on anything bigger or anything smaller than the child growing within me. On sunny days Lamprocles and the girls would take Sophroniscus out to run and play. Lamprocles and the older girls read while the younger girls chased after Sophroniscus.

Xanthippe, too, frequently remained inside. We began weaving together, although neither of us spoke as we worked. Our silence was more than a truce. It was a comfortable knowing and acceptance. The whole house breathed a deep, peaceful sigh.

Lamprocles felt slighted initially when I stopped going with them, but as the time to deliver the child approached, I could sense his growing excitement.

"May I assist you with this birth as well?" he asked one evening as we sat around the table eating. I assumed he was asking Socrates, but when I looked up, his eyes were on me. I turned to Socrates.

"It's entirely up to you, my dear," he said to me.

"Of course," I nodded my approval. "I'm counting on you and your birthing chair."

Lamprocles beamed. I watched as his expression changed from pleased to emboldened. He cleared his throat. "You know, I was thinking that you might like to have Mama Leda there beside you to comfort you, without the added distraction of supporting your arm."

Lamprocles paused, giving us a moment to absorb this suggestion and ask the obvious question.

I was happy to comply. "But you can only support one of my arms at a time, Lamprocles," I said. "Who will support my other arm as Socrates delivers the baby?"

"It just so happens I have someone in mind," Lamprocles replied. "She's very sympathetic and keeps her fingernails clean and well-trimmed."

Xanthippe frowned and looked at her fingernails. Socrates laughed. He appeared to be enjoying this discussion immensely.

"Do I know this person?" I asked. "Are you quite certain she'll want to assist?"

"Yes and yes," replied Lamprocles. "She's been an aspiring young midwife ever since you taught her to read."

A loud sigh of relief escaped from Xanthippe. "Are you telling us that Korinna wants to be a midwife?" she asked.

"She does," Lamprocles said. "In fact, she and I may someday become Athens' first male and female midwifery team. She's very bright, you know."

I nodded. "Korinna will make a wonderful assistant."

"Well, then," said Socrates, "it's all settled."

For the first time in my life everything did feel settled. Korinna began joining us at the table for our evening meal. With her came a new feeling of warmth and contentment. I patted the child in my belly as I watched the people I loved most eating and talking and laughing. *This is your family.*

It never occurred to me that an immense calmness might precede the greatest storm.

The child growing with me turned out to be another son. We named him Menexenus, meaning a foreigner who remains stead fast. This, too, reminded me of Aspasia. I once heard Socrates say that Aspasia's only crime was not having been born in Athens. She was a foreigner by birth, and although she'd lived most of her life in this country, her body, mind and spirit would always be strangely exotic.

News of Aspasia's death came late in the winter, soon after Menexenus' birth. Socrates and Lamprocles and even Xanthippe and Korinna joined the mourners in the funeral procession, but I stayed home with the children.

"Are you sure you won't join us?" Xanthippe asked. "Mama Leda can care for Sophroniscus and the baby, or you can even bring Menexenus with you. Korinna and I will help."

I shook my head. "It is best I stay home."

"Do you want me to stay with you?" asked Xanthippe.

"No, you go," I replied. "Go and mourn for Athens. Mama Leda will be here with me. While you are mourning, I will celebrate Aspasia's life and the memories I have of her."

30

ASPASIA'S DEATH SEEMED to spark a new debate on piety in Athens. Should she be honored as the wife of Pericles or should she have been brought to trial on charges of impiety as Aristophanes had suggested in *The Acharnians?*

One evening at dinner Lamprocles seemed particularly disturbed.

"What can they do?" Socrates asked. "Aspasia is dead."

"It's not Aspasia I'm worried about," retorted Lamprocles. He slammed his fists on the table and pushed himself away.

Xanthippe and Korinna looked genuinely startled. Socrates eyes were full of love and his face expressed complete tranquility. Lamprocles waited for someone to address his concern.

Finally, I asked, "What is it that you are worried about, Lamprocles?"

Lamprocles stretched both hands out toward Socrates. "I am worried about Aspasia's student," he said.

Socrates nodded, and I felt my stomach tightening into a knot. "What would you have me do?" he asked Lamprocles.

"Stay home for a while," Lamprocles pleaded. "Enjoy some time with your family. That's what old men are supposed to do, isn't it?"

Socrates laughed. "So I'm a useless old man, am I?"

"It's not funny." Lamprocles looked down and shook his head. When he looked up again, tears filled his eyes.

"I am old," Socrates agreed. "Too old to change."

"But there are rumors of men hoping to make a name for themselves by bringing charges against you," said Lamprocles. "If you continue to teach in the Agora, it will only encourage them."

"Charges of impiety?" I asked.

Lamprocles nodded. "For corrupting the youth of Athens."

"I'm far from dead," said Socrates, "but what can they possibly do to me now to rob me of the life I've chosen?"

"Imprison you!" exclaimed Lamprocles.

"Let them. They can provide me with free room and board for life, exactly as they do for our greatest athletes and generals," replied Socrates, his eyes gleaming.

"Or put you to death," I whispered. My own eyes filled with tears.

"My dear, I am nearly 70 years old." Socrates slipped his hand under the table and gave mine a squeeze. "If they want to kill me, they better hurry up about it before the gods beat them to it!"

Lamprocles held his head in his hands, elbows on the table. "What can we say or do to persuade you to stop?"

"Nothing," replied Socrates. He rose to his feet. "I did not abandon my post in battle, and I will not abandon it now." With both hands on the table, Socrates leaned in toward Lamprocles. "As long as I have breath to speak, I will continue to question anyone who says he has or seeks wisdom."

"Why?" asked Lamprocles. "What's the point?"

"It's who I am," said Socrates. "It's what the gods have called me to do." He shrugged his shoulders.

"But must you directly confront those in power in the process?" asked Lamprocles. He stood to face his father. For the first time I realized how much taller Lamprocles was than Socrates now. "There are plenty of people who like talking with you and want to learn from you." Lamprocles paced around the table. "Just talk to them for a while and leave the sophists and politicians to their own foolishness."

Socrates walked over to Lamprocles and placed a hand on his shoulder. A quiet sob passed through Lamprocles' lips. "Lamprocles," Socrates said tenderly, "I do not seek people out. They come to me. Wherever I am, they will come."

"Not if they don't know where to find you," said Lamprocles. His voice sounded so strained. There were tears in his eyes. I blinked back my own tears. Only Socrates' eyes were clear.

"Would you have me hiding like a coward?" Socrates embraced Lamprocles, who began to sob freely. Tears streamed down my cheeks as well. I could hear Korinna crying and even sniffles coming from Xanthippe. Socrates held Lamprocles close and patted him on the back. "I was born a citizen of Athens, and I will die a citizen of Athens. In the meantime, I will live like a true Athenian."

It wasn't long before Lamprocles' fears materialized. One afternoon Lamprocles returned early from the Agora without Socrates. "They've charged him," he told us.

A silent scream erupted within me. "Who?" I asked. "Who has made the accusation?"

"Meletus," said Lamprocles.

"Meletus!" exclaimed Xanthippe. "Who is this Meletus? I've never even heard of him!"

"He's some religious fanatic who calls himself a poet," Lamprocles replied. "A nobody really. A puppet."

The scream reached into my mind, strangling my thoughts.

"Whose puppet?" asked Korinna.

"I'm pretty sure Anytus is behind this," said Lamprocles, "only he's too afraid to bring formal accusations himself in case it should prove unpopular in the end."

"Anytus is a coward and a traitor!" Xanthippe spat on the ground. "He'll probably bribe the jury to convict Socrates the same way he bribed his jury to acquit him when he was charged with treason."

"Lamprocles," I whispered. "Take me to the public notice board so that I can see the charges myself."

Lamprocles nodded. "What about Menexenus?" he pointed to the child sleeping in my arms. *My child. I forgot about my child.*

Xanthippe gently lifted the infant from my arms. "Go," she told me. "Go and read the accusations for yourself. Mama Leda and I will take care of the baby and Sophroniscus."

"Shall I come with you?" Korinna asked me.

I stared at her blankly. The screaming inside me was growing louder. I could barely comprehend her words. She turned to Lamprocles, who nodded.

"Yes, come with us," he instructed her. And with that we set off to the Agora.

We walked for an eternity. Lamprocles and Korinna talked quietly between themselves. Occasionally, Lamprocles would raise his voice, and I could hear the battle raging within him. But it all felt so distant from me.

I tried to ignore the silent scream, but every effort to resist it only seemed to make it worse. Part of me recognized this scream. In fact, it had lived within me as long as I could remember. Yet like the clatter of the marketplace, it had always remained in the background and never held my full attention.

When did the screaming stop? Why did it start again so suddenly and so ferociously? How can I make it stop? The more I tried to stop it, the more ferocious it became, until I felt as if I might go mad. *No—just breathe.*

This last thought brought me back to reality and reduced the terrorizing scream to a dull roar as we entered the Agora and approached the statues of the Eponymous Heroes. There, posted outside the temple that housed the city archives, was a whitened board posted for public notice.

"There it is," said Lamprocles pointing to the public notice board. "Meletus presented the formal accusations to King Archon who ordered that they be written on this board and posted for all to see."

Meletus, citizen of Athens, hereby charges Socrates, citizen of Athens, with the following crime against the state and the gods of Athens: Impiety, to wit: not believing in the gods of Athens, believing instead in other spiritual things; and corrupting the young men of Athens. The penalty demanded is death.

A jury of 500 Athenian citizens shall assemble to determine the truth in this matter and dispense justice as required.

"Absurd!" I heard the voice of Plato behind me. "Utterly ridiculous!"

31

"FOR ONCE I agree with you, Plato" replied Lamprocles. "These charges couldn't be further from the truth."

"Meletus is a fool," said Plato. "You know who is behind this, don't you?"

Lamprocles nodded. "Anytus."

"Anytus and Lycon," Plato replied. "Let them call their own sons who both love Socrates dearly and ask them if Socrates corrupted them."

Lamprocles just shook his head. Korinna placed her hand on his back to calm him.

"I'll testify for him," said Plato with genuine conviction.

"A fat lot of good that will do," retorted Lamprocles. He stepped away from Korinna, moving closer to Plato. "Everyone still remembers you as the friend and family of the Thirty Tyrants." Lamprocles voice grew louder and his face flushed. "You and Alcibiades and Xenophon . . . Spartan lovers, all of you. If you care at all about my father, you'll not do him any favors."

Plato turned to me. "Perhaps when the jury sees his beautiful young wife and young sons, they will show him mercy."

"You say that as if you think I'm still a child." Lamprocles' anger seethed with every word.

"And you are not?" Plato laughed a spiteful laugh. "Perhaps you plan to save him yourself."

Lamprocles clenched his jaw and squared his shoulders with Plato's. He shifted his weight, readying himself for an attack. At 18, Lamprocles had grown tall and strong, but he would be no match for Plato in wrestling or in argument.

"Stop it, both of you!" I ordered. "Your fighting isn't going to help anyone." To my surprise they each took a step backward and turned to me. Lamprocles scowled and crossed his arms.

"I apologize," Plato said to me. His plaintiff expression and pleading eyes surprised me. "I know that this must be just as upsetting to you as it is to me, probably more so." He turned to Lamprocles. "I am sorry. I will help in any way I can, even if it means doing nothing."

"Where is Socrates?" I asked.

"Under his favorite laurel tree, where else?" Plato motioned toward the marketplace. "He's acting as if nothing is wrong."

I went to find Socrates. Korinna walked beside me. Plato and Lamprocles followed. I could hear them discussing the charges behind me. Whenever one would start to raise his voice, the other would shush him. We found Socrates surrounded by an even greater number of young men than usual.

I called to Socrates as I made my way through the crowd. "Your notoriety seems to have increased your popularity," I said.

"Myrto!" he exclaimed. "How lovely that you and Korinna can join us!" He motioned for us to come and sit next to him. "Plato, Lamprocles, welcome."

I took my place beside him, but I longed to talk to him alone, not as part of a crowd.

"We were just discussing piety," Socrates said. "We agreed that it applies to everything the gods love, but now we can't seem to decide whether something is pious because the gods love it or whether the gods love it because it is pious."

I nodded.

Plato gave me a mischievous grin before raising his own question. "It seems to me that the gods do not always love the same things. Must all of the gods love something for it to be pious or is the love of one god sufficient?"

This created quite a stir, but the discussion continued without my participation or attention. Instead, I watched my husband, so lively and energetic in his pursuit of wisdom and truth. I watched how the countenance of a young man could change so quickly from determined to puzzled, then show a sudden flash of understanding that eventually gave way to confusion as he considered each additional question. *This is Socrates. This is what he does. Asking him to stop would be a punishment worse than death.*

I imagined Socrates locked in a cell inside the State Prison just outside the Agora along the street leading to the Piraeus Gate. *Would crowds gather there as well? As long as they do, Socrates will be happy... happy to have free room and board while he continues his philosophy, doing exactly what the gods have ordained.*

That night when we were finally alone in bed in the darkness, I asked him the question that was on my heart. "Do you think that the jury will acquit you?"

"I don't know," he replied. He nestled up beside me, and held me close in his arms. "Even if they convict me, it will be up to the jury to decide what sentence they want to impose."

"I'm scared," I confessed. I wanted to talk to him about the silent scream in my head.

"I know," he whispered.

"I feel waves of emotion crashing inside me. There's a roar that seems to grow louder in the silence." My throat tightened and my eyes filled with tears.

Socrates kissed my forehead. "It sounds like a storm is brewing inside you."

"The only place I feel safe is in your arms." I buried my head in his chest and cried. Socrates held me gently and let the storm run its course.

When I could once again breathe freely I asked, "What about you? Aren't you at least worried about the accusations?"

"I'm feeling strangely calm," he replied. "My spirit usually gives me a strong sign when I should seek a different direction. I've avoided many calamities by paying attention to this inner knowing."

"What is your spirit telling you now?"

"Nothing," he replied. "My spirit is telling me nothing."

"Is that bad?" I asked, sitting up.

"On the contrary," Socrates explained, "nothing is good."

The double meaning of these words sent a shiver down my spine. "Nothing is good makes it sound like everything is bad." Socrates reached for my hand and pulled me back beside him.

"Everything is definitely not bad, Myrto," said Socrates. "Everything is good."

"Nothing is good. Everything is good. How can that be?" I whispered.

Socrates yawned. "It just is, my love." Before long, Socrates' breaths became heavy and turned to soft snores.

Nothing is good. Everything is good . . . Everything is nothing. That's it. Everything is nothing, and nothing is everything.

This somehow made perfect sense as I drifted off to sleep.

32

THE MORNING OF the trial I rubbed every last drop of the oil from my alabaster jar into Socrates' skin. He was sitting on the edge of our bed, and Menexenus was still sleeping in the middle of the bed. "Do you want me there?" I asked as I massaged his hands.

Socrates watched my hands at work for a moment. When I ran my palm over his, he clasped my hand and held it. "Do you want to be there?" he asked.

I waited for him to look up. "I want you to know that I love you and that I would do anything for you," I replied, holding both his gaze and his hand.

He raised my hand to his lips. I felt the warmth of his breath as he kissed the back of my hand. "I'm not asking you to do anything."

I sat on the bed beside him. Menexenus stirred. "My head wants to see and hear for myself," I said, "but my heart wants nothing to do with your accusers and their lies."

I lifted Menexenus to my breast so that he could nurse. "Can I stand by your side throughout the trial?"

Socrates shook his head. "I must stand alone."

I rocked Menexenus back and forth gently. "Can I sit on the jury and cast a vote for your innocence?"

Socrates chuckled. "Athena will cast her vote for acquittal."

"Athena only gets to vote in case of a tie," I replied. "If half of the jurors were women, I should think that would be enough. I do not trust a jury made up only of men."

Socrates laughed. "I do not have the luxury of choosing my accusers or my jury," said Socrates. "Do you think a jury of Amazon women would acquit?" His impish grin made me laugh, too.

"Five hundred Amazon women and Athena would do wonders for Athens!" I exclaimed. The idea of a government run entirely by women warriors amused us both greatly, and we laughed even harder. We laughed until we cried.

I looked at my husband and remembered how his features had struck me as odd the first time I saw him. But knowing him, living with him, laughing with him, and loving him had created an attraction beyond any I could have imagined. *And now . . . what will become of us?*

"Seriously, Socrates," I said, "are you prepared to give a speech in your own defense?"

"Seriously?" asked Socrates. "I try not to take myself too seriously, but I can assure you that I've lived my whole life preparing for this."

"What will you say?" I asked, wiping the last of the tears from my eyes.

"I honestly don't know," he replied. "Maybe nothing." He stood and readied himself to go.

Sometimes nothing is everything.

"One thing you can be sure of, though," Socrates said. He bent down and kissed Menexenus on the forehead before kissing me on the lips. "I'll make no apologies for who I am or the life I've lived."

I carried Menexenus with me as we went out to greet the rest of the household. Lamprocles, Xanthippe and Korinna were sitting around the table eating figs and talking quietly.

Lamprocles jumped to his feet when he saw us. "You must get ready," Lamprocles said to me. He reached out to take Menexenus from me. "It's time to go."

"I'm not going," I replied.

Lamprocles looked stunned. "How can you just not go?" Lamprocles asked throwing his outstretched hands up. "How can you not want to be there for him?"

"If he wanted me there, I would go," I replied.

Socrates cleared his throat. "You're talking about me as if I weren't here." He stood by the table and popped a fig in his mouth.

"I'm sorry, Father," replied Lamprocles, "but I thought Myrto would be there." Another look of bewilderment crossed his face. "Do you not wish for me to be there either?"

"Do you want to be there?" asked Socrates. He replaced the pit in his mouth with another fig.

"Yes, of course!" cried Lamprocles.

"Then I want you to be there," Socrates replied. He turned to Korinna and Xanthippe. "Would you like to join us?"

Korinna nodded. Xanthippe shook her head.

"Very well, then," Socrates said to Lamprocles and Korinna, "let's go." He kissed both Xanthippe and me on the cheek before he left.

As soon as they were gone, Xanthippe motioned to me to sit beside her. "Are you sure you do not wish to go?" she asked. She pushed a plate of bread and figs toward me.

I shook my head. "There's nothing I can do," I replied. "And I would rather do nothing here in peace than be part of an ugly crowd of confusion."

"But sometimes having a wife and children there can make a difference," Xanthippe said. "Sometimes the jurors feel sympathetic and their verdict is less harsh."

Again I shook my head. I shifted Menexenus gently to my other arm.

"I think you should go," Xanthippe said finally.

"You go," I replied. "You were his wife long before I came along."

Xanthippe slapped the table and cackled. "Me! I've never aroused sympathy in anyone."

The loud noise startled the baby, and he began to cry. I walked with him, bouncing him to soothe him. "Shhh," I whispered in his ear.

"See," cried Xanthippe. "I irritate people even more than Socrates does!" Xanthippe looked exasperated. "Anything I do will only make matters worse."

"Then stay here with me. We will do nothing together."

Xanthippe sighed heavily and held her head in her hands.

Xanthippe did not know how to do nothing. I could hear her anxiously whispering prayers to Zeus, Apollo, Hera and Athena throughout the day. Mama Leda and the girls took care of Sophroniscus.

I cradled Menexenus in my arms all day. As long as I held him in my arms, there was no silent scream. I comforted myself by comforting him.

The afternoon grew long, and Xanthippe became even more fretful. They did not return even at sunset. "Why aren't they back yet?" Xanthippe asked no one in particular time and time again.

We knew. We both knew, but the knowing affected us differently. I became increasingly calm and aware. Xanthippe became increasingly agitated and distracted.

It was very late when Lamprocles and Korinna returned. Xanthippe and I were in the courtyard. She was pacing; I was rocking Menexenus.

"Where is Socrates?" Xanthippe asked when it became apparent that he was not with them.

Lamprocles embraced her, but said nothing. His eyes were glassy and swollen.

"Where is Socrates?" Xanthippe asked again.

Finally, Lamprocles replied, "He is in prison." His voice sounded much older than it had this morning.

Xanthippe pushed away from his embrace, but Lamprocles did not release her.

"Guilty?" Xanthippe asked. "They found him guilty?"

Korinna nodded. "Guilty," she said. "Two hundred and eighty votes for guilty and two hundred twenty votes for acquittal." She looked at me. "If only thirty more men had voted to acquit . . . " She could not finish the thought. Her eyes, too, were puffy and red. She came and sat beside me.

"And the penalty?" asked Xanthippe. "Surely if so many voted to acquit, they must have been lenient in their punishment."

Lamprocles shook his head. "Once they convicted him, an even greater number voted for a penalty of death." Xanthippe groaned deeply and fell limp in Lamprocles' embrace. He brought her over to Korinna and me and sat her gently between us.

"How?" I asked. "How will he die?"

"Poison hemlock," Korinna said softly.

"When?" I asked.

"I don't know," Lamprocles replied. "The ship in honor of Theseus has only just set sail on its annual mission to Delos. Athens will not risk angering the gods by executing anyone before the ship returns."

"And in the meantime?" I asked.

"He'll remain in the state prison," replied Lamprocles.

Korinna nodded. "The guards put him in the largest cell. They said that we can visit whenever we like. Crito was still with him when we left."

"Then I will go see him now," I said.

"Now?" cried Lamprocles and Xanthippe in unison.

"At this hour?" Xanthippe asked.

"Wouldn't it be better to wait until tomorrow morning?" asked Lamprocles. "He'll be there for days, maybe even another month depending upon the winds."

"Good," I replied. "I can take Sophroniscus to see him later." I turned to Korinna. "Would you prepare a satchel of wine and food for me to take with me while I put Menexenus in a sling and get ready to go?" Korinna nodded and went off to do as I asked.

Once I was ready, I turned to Xanthippe. "Do you wish to see him tonight?" I asked.

"Not tonight," she said. "I will go with Lamprocles tomorrow."

Lamprocles looked torn. He was exhausted and his mother needed him, yet I could see that he wanted to go with me.

"Let me walk with you," said Korinna. "I will carry the satchel and a torch."

171

Lamprocles nodded his approval. "At least let Korinna walk with you. The night is too black for you to walk alone in the darkness."

33

SOCRATES DID NOT seem at all surprised to see us. I greeted him with a kiss. He embraced me and Menexenus in a single hug.

He turned to Korinna. "Thank you for bringing them to me safely." Korinna's eyelids looked heavy. Socrates asked the guard if there was a bed where she might sleep. He seemed anxious to accommodate Socrates in every way. Korinna and Menexenus were soon nestled snugly into a bed in the guards' quarters.

Socrates' cell was actually quite large and well-furnished. "I've never heard of anyone having a couch or a table and chairs in prison," I said.

"Isn't it lovely?" said Socrates. "Crito had them brought in."

"Are you hungry?" I asked. "Korinna packed some food and wine for us." I felt hunger in my own stomach from not having eaten all day. I began to spread out a meal on the table for us.

"I think I'm going to like it here," said Socrates. He breathed in deeply and stretched his arms out as if embracing his prison cell. "It's very conveniently located near the Agora, don't you think?"

I sighed. "Very convenient." I seated myself at the table. Socrates pulled up a chair and joined me.

Socrates talked as we ate, telling me not about his trial, but instead about a conversation he had with a young man named Euthyphro outside the court shortly before his trial began.

"Imagine this," he said. "Just as I was contemplating for myself what piety really is, I ran into Euthyphro who understands piety so well that he had just filed murder charges against his own father."

"Against his own father?" I asked. "How can that be pious? His father must have killed his mother or grandfather for a son to bring such charges!"

"That's what I thought," said Socrates. He drank from the wineskin and then offered it to me. "But Euthyphro said it makes no difference whether the victim is a stranger or relative. Justice demands that the murderer be prosecuted."

I shrugged my shoulders and kept eating. Socrates continued his tale.

"In fact, the victim in this case was a servant, and a murderer himself. Euthyphro's father had him bound and held after the servant had killed a household slave in drunken anger."

"How did Euthyphro's father kill him?" I asked between bites.

"He didn't," Socrates replied. "He sent a messenger to ask the priest what he should do with the servant, and the servant died of neglect before the messenger returned."

"I can't imagine a son bringing murder charges against his own father in those circumstances," I said. By this time I had eaten my fill, and my body was aching to lie down.

"By Zeus, that's what I thought!" Socrates exclaimed. "So I asked him, 'Are you so confident in your knowledge of the divine, and of piety and impiety, that you have no fear of bringing such charges against your own father?' And do you know what he said?"

I shook my head.

"He assured me that piety demanded a good son to prosecute his father to the fullest extent allowed by the law," Socrates replied. Socrates took my hand and walked me from the table over to the couch to lie down. He extinguished the lamps before lying down beside me.

I yawned and stretched. "I don't understand," I said.

"Nor do I," Socrates admitted. "Apparently, I don't understand piety at all." He sighed. "But that's one good thing about you and me—at least we know that we don't know."

Socrates was still talking about Euthyphro and piety as I drifted off to sleep.

I dreamed that I was sitting alone in a dark prison cell. I could hear Socrates' voice behind me and see his shadow on the wall in front of me. I tried to turn around, but I could not move. I called out to him to come and sit beside me, but he did not come. I called out again, this time more loudly. A jailer came and told me to quiet down.

"Where is Socrates?" I asked him.

"Socrates is dead," he replied.

"He can't be!" I exclaimed. "I just heard him. I just saw his shadow on the wall before me."

"Your mind is playing tricks on you," said the jailer. "Go back to sleep."

"I cannot sleep," I cried. "I must find Socrates."

"You are dreaming," said the jailer. "Socrates is dead."

I awoke with a start. I was dreaming. Socrates was alive, right there beside me. *But for how much longer?*

A streak of sunlight streamed into the room through a tiny window near the ceiling. I could see Socrates still sleeping beside me. I got up to check on Korinna and Menexenus. I lifted my child from the bed. Korinna stirred.

The jailer peeked his head in the room and asked if everything was all right.

"Yes, thank you," I replied. "Are jailers always so kind?"

The jailer smiled. "We have never had a prisoner like Socrates. He is the noblest, the gentlest and the best man who has ever come here."

Korinna and I walked back to Socrates' cell together. Crito and several others were already beginning to gather there.

"I must go now," I told Socrates. "Xanthippe and Lamprocles will be here later, and I'll bring Sophroniscus to see you as well."

Socrates nodded and kissed me goodbye.

"He seems awfully content for a man just sentenced to die," said Korinna as we walked home together.

Over the next several days we settled into a routine. I spent the days at home and the nights with Socrates. Usually I would take Menexenus with me, but occasionally I would not. Lamprocles spent every day with Socrates. Xanthippe and Korinna would take Sophroniscus for a short visit every couple of days.

Socrates had very little time to himself, but when he did he occupied himself by composing poetry. Most of his poems honored Apollo, but some transformed Aesop's fables into verse. My favorite went something like this:

The Dog and the Bone

One day a dog was digging for a bone,
And came upon the best he'd ever seen.
So greedily he snatched it for his own.
He held it in his paws and licked it clean.

Head high and trophy safely clenched in jaw
He trotted homeward, fully satisfied.
But as he crossed a bridge, beneath he saw
Another dog and bone that walked in stride.

That bone below—the grandest of them all!
Our hero barked and leapt in to the stream,
The bone he had forgotten in the fall,
The bone he sought a hopeless, splashing dream.

The one who chases treasure out of greed,
May soon wake up to find himself in need.

"You should write your poems down," I told him.

"You know, Myrto, writing shares a strange feature with painting," he replied. "A painting stands there looking as if it were alive, but if you ask it anything, it remains silent."

"It's art, Socrates," I replied. "A good painting communicates the inspiration of the gods."

Socrates shook his head. "The highest form of art for me is philosophy."

"So write about philosophy," I suggested.

"But if I write about philosophy and my words appear to have some understanding, what happens when someone wants to learn more? My words would just say the same thing over and over again like an imbecile." Socrates made a funny face and tilted his head back and forth like an idiot.

"That's true," I conceded, "but think of all the people who might read those words and learn from them."

"Yes, but my words would roam about everywhere reaching indiscriminately those with understanding and those without," said Socrates. Socrates walked his fingers up and down my legs.

"And what if I learned that something I wrote was not entirely true?" Socrates said, walking his fingers up my arm. "My writings would still say the same things over and over, true or untrue." He walked his fingers up my neck and tapped my head. "Think about it," he said. He kissed my head where he had tapped. "No, thank you. I'll leave the writing to those who are convinced of their knowledge or inspired by the muses."

34

SOCRATES AND I spent every night together knowing it could be our last. We didn't talk about people or politics. We didn't talk about the past or the future. We talked about virtues and ideas—wisdom and goodness and justice in all of their forms, and whether any single virtue could stand apart from the others. We lived only in the present, enjoying the presence of one another.

I was a mother by day and a wife by night. Only when I was alone with Socrates in prison, I never thought of him as my husband or of myself as his wife. He was just Socrates, and I was just Myrto. We were friends and lovers and soul mates.

We spent hours sitting together on the couch talking about life and love. Socrates held me close in his arms, but our closeness was in mind and spirit as well as in body. "I love you," I whispered. He kissed me tenderly.

"What is love, Myrto?" he asked.

"Love is the way I feel about you, Socrates."

"Is love only a feeling, or is it more than just a feeling?" he asked.

"It's more than just a feeling," I replied. "It's also knowing and being known."

"And what is it that you know?" Socrates asked.

"That our love cannot be contained in your body or mine, or even in the bodies of our children," I said. "And that even when your body is no longer here with us, the love will live on in my heart."

Socrates nodded. "So is love mortal or immortal?"

"Perhaps love is the one immortal thing that a mortal animal can do," I said.

Socrates stroked my hair. "Do all mortal animals seek to be immortal or is it only humans who dream of becoming gods?"

"Don't all animals seek immortality?" I asked. "Isn't that why wild animals mate and nurture their young, even to the point of dying to protect their weaker offspring?"

"I suppose it is," Socrates mused. "Are you suggesting that immortality is a cycle?" He kissed me on the forehead and motioned for me to have a seat at the table. Each day a new abundance of food and wine and delicacies appeared in Socrates' cell.

I followed him to the feast. "For the gods immortality means always being the same in every way," I said, "but for us, life perpetuates itself in cycles. Immortality is more like aging and departing, but leaving behind something new in our place."

Socrates tore a leavened barley cake into two portions and gave me one.

"Even our bodies are constantly growing and aging," I continued. "New skin replaces old skin; new hairs replace the hairs that fall out."

Socrates nodded. He poured us each a cup of wine and took a drink.

"Just look at this old body," he said. "I was once an infant like Menexenus, and a toddler like Sophroniscus and a strong young man like Lamprocles. Now I am older than my father or his father before him. Yet I have always been Socrates, even as I've grown and changed."

I took his hand in mine. "That is the Socrates I love," I told him. "Your spirit—the essence of who you really are."

I broke off a small piece of the barley cake and chewed it slowly. I washed it down with a sip of wine.

"That is the Socrates that will live forever in my heart and in the hearts of all those who know you and love you," I said.

"And yet there are many who don't find me very lovable," said Socrates.

"They are afraid of you," I replied. "Your questions unravel the stories they tell themselves and everyone else."

"So are those who don't love me unlovable?" Socrates asked. He unfolded a cloth filled with dried fish.

"I don't know," I said. I ate several of the fish, enjoying their saltiness and the thirst they created in my mouth.

"But I don't think it's worth my time and energy to hate them," I said. I poured some water into my wine and swirled it with my finger before taking several large swallows.

"It's one thing not to hate them," said Socrates, "but are they lovable?"

"Surely someone loves them," I replied. I lifted my cup toward the lamp and watched the flame's reflection dancing on a sea of redness. "When I first met Xanthippe I thought she was unlovable," I reflected.

"And now?" Socrates asked.

"And now I love her," I said. The words surprised me as they passed my lips, but I knew they were true. "She is part of Lamprocles, part of you, and part of the life I have come to love." I looked deeply into Socrates' eyes and felt the strength of his love—a love

181

for all that is good inextricably bound to a belief that the good lives in all of us. "Xanthippe is part of me now," I told him.

"Only now?" asked Socrates.

I shook my head. "Not only this present moment. Always."

"Always goes in both directions, you know," replied Socrates.

"What are you saying?" I asked.

"Always has no beginning and no end. Always just is."

"Like now," I said smiling. I took another drink of wine.

"Exactly," said Socrates.

"That must be your secret to happiness, Socrates," I said. "You always surround yourself with love by loving everything around you."

"It's true," he replied. "People can never be unlovable if we choose to love them."

"And it doesn't matter if they love us in return?" I asked.

"What do you think?" asked Socrates.

"Maybe love does not come from being loved, but from loving," I said.

Socrates nodded. "That would be true love—divine love."

"A love that reaches beyond human bodies and human understanding," I said thinking aloud. "Could it be that love is the spirit that comes from the gods and bridges the gap between mortality and immortality?"

Socrates smiled. "Where do you suppose our desire for immortality comes from?" asked Socrates. "Do we really desire to be forever unchanging like the gods?"

I leaned back in my chair and ran my hands through my hair. Aspasia appeared in my mind's eye. I stood and walked over to the couch as if I were attempting to escape my own thoughts. I shook my head and sat down. "Sometimes I think that we have created the gods in our own image because we cannot even imagine a world where everything stays the same."

Socrates came and sat beside me. "My own thoughts scare me sometimes," I confessed. "Could it be that all of our images, everything around us that we believe to be real, are but illusions?"

"What is real, Myrto?" Socrates asked. "What do you really know for sure?"

"I know that I am Myrto," I replied. "I am real, and I choose to love."

"That is enough to carry you through this world and into the next," said Socrates.

35

I WALKED TO the prison at sunset and back home at sunrise. I was always walking against the crowds. At first people stared at me. I could feel them pointing and talking. After a while, the people disappeared into clouds of fog, the fog that I walked through each morning to get to my children and each evening to get to Socrates.

One evening as I walked to the prison, I heard a voice calling me from the fog. "Myrto! Wait!"

It was Plato. I did not want to wait. I wanted to continue walking through the fog to Socrates.

Plato caught up to me and walked beside me. "Please, Myrto, I need to talk with you."

I kept walking. "About what?" I asked.

"About the future," he said.

"My only plans for the future are to spend this night with Socrates," I replied. I walked faster.

"I know," said Plato, keeping pace with me. "But it's been nearly a month since . . . " His voice trailed off. "I mean," he began again, "the ship will be returning from Delos any day."

"But it did not return today, did it?" I asked in a tone more assertive than inquiring.

"No," replied Plato softly. "The ship did not return today."

"Then I will spend this night with Socrates and worry about tomorrow when the time comes." We were approaching the Street of Marble Workers in the southwest corner of the Agora, almost to the prison.

"But I need to talk with you before the time comes," Plato said. He reached for my hand and held me back. "Please," he said. "Just sit and talk with me for a moment." He guided me over to a fountain and sat me on a wooden bench. "We need to make proper arrangements, Myrto."

I covered my face with my hands and shook my head. "No," I said looking back up at him. "Lamprocles and Xanthippe will make all of the necessary arrangements."

"I'm not talking about Socrates' funeral, Myrto." Plato placed his hand under my chin and slowly lifted my head. I did not resist. Soon my eyes met his. I felt a lump forming in my throat and tears gathering in my eyes.

"I'm talking about your future, Myrto," said Plato. A future for you and for Sophroniscus and Menexenus."

A chill ran up my spine. "I . . . I don't understand," I stammered. For the first time in weeks I could hear the silent scream burst out within me.

"I have asked Socrates for your hand in marriage," Plato said. "Not right away, of course." He rushed on. "There would need to be a proper period of mourning. But after that, he has given us his blessing to marry."

My heart pounded and my mind raced. I could hear and feel the roar. I shook my head. "I don't know," I said finally.

"I know." Plato replied. "That is why I wanted to talk to you now, so that you could ask Socrates yourself." He raised his eyebrows and gave me a hopeful look. He reached for my hand and his eyes filled with tears. "I love you, Myrto. From the first moment I saw you, I've loved you." He held both of my hands in his. "We are young. Our whole lives lie ahead."

I felt so bewildered. I could not respond. "Sophroniscus," I whispered. "Menexenus."

"I would love them and raise them like my own sons," Plato promised. "I'm not asking you to be my servant, Myrto. I'm asking you to be my partner." Plato stood and began to pace as he talked.

"Together we could rebuild Athens. We would be like Pericles and Aspasia, only we would both be citizens and equal partners. Forget democracy and tyrants and kings. Athens needs a republic, and we could build it together. We would rule justly and with integrity."

He came back and sat beside me. "I know I'm rambling," he said. "I know now is not the time to discuss details, and I'm not asking for your answer now either. I'm only asking that you think about your future and the future of your sons. If you have any doubts, talk to Socrates."

"Socrates," I said. "Yes, I must go to Socrates."

Plato stood and lifted me gently to my feet. "Go," he said quietly. "Go to Socrates."

When I arrived at the prison cell, a small crowd remained. Everyone sensed that the end drew near, and many did not know how to let go. Faced with Plato's proposal, I felt myself wanting to cling to Socrates as well. I left the group in the cell, walked down the corridor and seated myself in the large courtyard at the far end of the prison.

A young prison guard followed me down the corridor. The number of jailers increased with the number of passing days and the growing crowds. All of them treated me kindly. "Is there anything I can get for you, ma'am?" asked the guard.

"No, thank you," I replied. I walked around the courtyard until I came upon a patch of myrtle.

"Would you like me to let you know when all of the men have gone?" the guard asked.

"You are very thoughtful," I said. "Yes, please let me know once Socrates is alone." He nodded and returned to his post by Socrates' cell.

As the last rays of daylight disappeared from the sky, a crescent moon shone brightly overhead. I sat on the edge of the courtroom fountain and tried to think of nothing. I breathed deeply and felt the roar within me subside a bit. *What am I feeling? Anger. Why am I angry? Plato! He thinks he can replace Socrates!*

I dipped my hand in the fountain, dispelling the reflection of my image into the moon's shimmering light. If the gods had asked me to choose between Plato and Socrates on my wedding night, there would have been no contest.

Plato is so much younger and more physically attractive. And he is charming. He is the one who awakened my first true desire—the desire to read.

Plato's wife would never have to worry about having her and her children's daily needs provided. She would have many slaves and servants.

I can choose to love Plato. I do love Plato. I will always love him as a friend and brother, but I can never love him as I have loved Socrates.

"Hello, my love," Socrates' voice interrupted my thoughts.

I turned and ran to his arms. "You are out of your cell!" I exclaimed. I realized I was crying and blotted my eyes with the sleeve of my tunic.

Socrates nodded. "Crito has paid all of the jailers handsomely. They've given me ample opportunities to escape."

"And will you?" I asked. At that moment I wanted only to walk out together, find Sophroniscus and Menexenus, and leave Athens forever.

"You know I cannot," replied Socrates. "I am an Athenian. Crito can pay to open the prison cell, but he cannot purchase my freedom as a citizen of Athens."

Socrates took my hand, and we walked around the courtyard together. "It does feel good to walk, even if we are going nowhere," Socrates commented as we continued to walk the circle.

"Plato stopped me on my way here tonight," I said. "He told me he had talked to you about your wishes once you are gone."

"Once I am gone, I will have no wishes," Socrates said.

"But Plato said that you wish for him to marry me and raise your sons after you are gone," I told him.

"Those are Plato's wishes, not mine," replied Socrates.

I sighed loudly in exasperation. "So you do not want me to marry Plato?" I asked. I found myself walking more abruptly and pulling Socrates along with me.

"All I want is for you to be happy," said Socrates.

"And you think your dying and my marrying Plato will make me happy?" I stepped in front of him, blocking his path and placing my closed fists on his chest between us.

"Plato is not happy about my dying." Socrates covered my fists with his hands and bent down to kiss each one individually. "But if I must die, then Plato does want to marry you."

"I am not happy about your dying!" I cried. I drummed my fists on his chest, not wanting to hurt him, yet wanting him to feel my pain. Socrates put his arms around me and pulled me close.

"I cannot live in this body forever, Myrto," Socrates whispered in my ear. "When I am gone, I want you to find your own happiness."

"By marrying Plato?" I asked. My voice trembled. Tears ran down my cheeks and onto Socrates' prison garb.

"If that is what you want, then you have my blessing," he said. "Your life is entirely up to you."

"But it's not!" I argued. "A woman born in Athens has no legal standing apart from a man. It seems marrying Plato would solve all of my problems."

"Marriage is never the answer to anyone's problems." Socrates took my hand and led me back to his prison cell. "You know, Aspasia seemed to do just fine even after the death of Pericles and the death of Lysicles." He motioned for me to sit on a couch beside him.

"But she was a foreigner, not a woman born in Athens," I countered, moving to the far end of the couch and keeping some distance between us.

"Yes," agreed Socrates, "but she was confronted with the same customs you are, and the same issues of propriety that seek to restrain us all."

I sat in silence, recalling the fear I felt when Father died, wondering what would become of me. "When Father died, you and my brother Aristides made arrangements for me according to custom. You never said I had a choice."

Socrates reached out to give me comfort. "You never asked."

My frustration drove me to my feet, and I began pacing before my husband. He dropped his hands in his lap. "And now that you know you have a choice, you seem angry that you must decide for yourself."

"I am angry!" I cried. "I'm angry at you for dying. I'm angry at Plato for wanting to marry me. I am angry at all of Athens for condemning you unjustly."

Socrates nodded. "Anger is a most appropriate response to injustice."

I waited for him to say more, but he did not. His simple acknowledgment and acceptance of my anger somehow worked to assuage it. I sat down right next to him and laid my head in his lap. "What am I going to do? It's not just me. I have to do what's best for Sophroniscus and Menexenus."

Socrates stroked the hair around my ear. "What's best for you will be best for our sons. You must be true to yourself, Myrto."

"I'm afraid," I whispered.

"I understand that fear." Socrates leaned down and kissed my head. "The courage it takes to be true to oneself is greater even than that of a man in combat or a woman in childbirth."

36

EVEN BEFORE DAWN the following morning, one of the jailers rapped lightly on the prison door. "The ship has been sighted just off the coast," he announced. Grief filled his voice. "It will surely dock today." He left us in silence.

We lay together, holding each other, full of life and love, for the last time. As dawn broke, my heart broke with it. I kissed my husband goodbye and wandered home, a lost soul.

Lamprocles saw me approaching and rushed to meet me. "I can see the sorrow in your every step," he cried.

I nodded. "The ship has returned." We held each other and cried shamelessly until there were no more tears inside either of us.

"I will not go back," I told Lamprocles.

He nodded. "I will take my mother and brothers to say our goodbyes."

In the days that followed, Sophroniscus and Menexenus were my salvation. They were too young to understand, and they needed me in the most ordinary ways. I viewed each moment through their eyes, gratefully partaking of their innocence and wonder. If what was best for me was best for them, then perhaps also what was best for them was best for me.

Xanthippe and Lamprocles fulfilled all the duties of a wife and son from burial rituals to public lamentations. I mourned privately in silence. I neither cut my hair nor tore my garments. When the children slept, I found myself contemplating nothing for long periods of time. There were no silent screams, no roaring tides of emotion. Instead, I discovered great healing in absolute nothingness.

After an appropriate passage of time, Plato came to call. Lamprocles greeted him coolly, and Xanthippe's invitation to pass through our front gate was less than welcoming.

"Let's go for a walk so that we may talk privately," Plato suggested.

I nodded and reached for my cloak.

Xanthippe nudged Lamprocles. "You will accompany them. Walk far enough behind them so that you cannot hear what they are saying, but do not let her out of your sight."

Plato looked offended, but I found myself smiling warmly.

We walked toward the River Illisus. At first we walked in silence with Plato looking back over his shoulder to keep Lamprocles at a distance.

"You look beautiful, Myrto," Plato said at last. I said nothing. Plato talked of all the goings on in the city since Socrates' death. "Most Athenians regret the execution of Socrates," he said. "They've commissioned a sculptor to set up a statue in his memory."

I laughed. "A cold, hard statue that will never question anyone," I said. "That is not how I would choose to honor his memory."

"But don't you see?" asked Plato. "You and I can do more than honor his memory. We can build his legacy."

"How?" I asked.

"The fields are ripe and ready for harvest," Plato said earnestly. Then he lowered his voice. "I have friends who can arrange for a small uprising. They will gladly assist us in establishing a truly just society in Athens."

"What is a truly just society?" I asked. "What does that even mean?"

"It means a republic, ruled by philosophers, men and women alike who understand political organization and how to educate young people on the precise nature of justice and virtue." Plato's voice grew louder as he attempted to persuade me. "Surely you agree that all people will have a better, happier life with just rulers than with unjust rulers."

"And where will Athens find such wise and just rulers?" I asked.

"I'm talking about us, Myrto. You and me together."

"Why us?" I asked.

"There is no one else!" Plato exclaimed. "No one loved Socrates like we did. Athens will embrace us, if only to absolve itself of Socrates' death."

"What about Lamprocles?" I asked. "Surely they would embrace Socrates' son over us."

Plato shook his head. "He's just now begun training as an ephebe." Plato looked back over his shoulder at Lamprocles. "It will be two years before he's a full citizen. The time to build a republic is now. Two years may be too late."

"No," I replied. "Talk to Lamprocles. I need to take care of my sons. My duty is to them, not to the Athenians who killed their father."

Plato took a deep breath. "Do you really think that Lamprocles is interested in government? I've heard he aspires to become a physician. I'm quite certain that we could arrange for him to become an apprentice to Hippocrates." He looked back at Lamprocles again and smiled. "Lamprocles could learn a lot from Hippocrates."

"Hippocrates could learn a lot from Lamprocles," I said.

Plato groaned. We were approaching the river. Plato motioned for us to have a seat on the bank.

"It's too soon, isn't it?" he said finally. "You're just not ready."

I shook my head. "It's not about timing," I told him. "I have no desire to rule anyone. That's your dream, not mine."

"No, Myrto," said Plato. "My dream is not to rule anyone. I saw how that kind of power turned my Uncle Charmides and my cousin Critias into tyrants." He leaned in toward me, and I caught a glimpse of the hope that had lighted his eyes the day I first met him. "My dream is for a just society. When our rulers fail to love wisdom, then it's time for those who love wisdom to become rulers."

I turned to watch the water running its course in the riverbed. So much had changed. I was not the same Myrto and he was not the same Plato that met in the marketplace years ago. Still, I recalled Socrates words from that day: "Is there anyone who loves wisdom and justice more than Plato?"

I looked again at Plato. He did love wisdom and justice. And Socrates. But loving the same things did not mean that we shared the same duty. "My duty is to my family," I told him again.

Plato reached out and gently lifted my chin to look me squarely in the eyes. "We could be family," he said. "Forget everything I said about governing and rulers. Just marry me. Marry me because I love you."

I could feel tears welling in the back of my eyes, so I lowered my head and closed them.

When I finally looked up, Plato said, "You do at least have some feelings for me, don't you, Myrto?" His eyes held mine, searching for the truth behind my tears. "I'm not asking you to love me the way you loved Socrates. I'm asking you to love me as a friend. Let's continue together in our pursuit of wisdom. In honor of Socrates."

I lay back on the bank and looked up into the sky. White fleecy clouds floated serenely above us, completely free from the world of problems far below them. They glided smoothly onward like a herd of winged rams. It was in this moment that I felt it for the first time: the courage to be myself, the desire to dream my own dreams and live my own life.

"I do have feeling for you, Plato," I confessed. "I love you as a friend and a brother."

"Then marry me," he replied. "Be my companion and my partner. I'll never bring up politics again."

"But what would you do with yourself all day?" I asked.

"We could build a school and educate young men and women alike," he replied.

I shook my head.

"What?" asked Plato.

"Nothing," I said.

"Tell me," Plato urged.

"I know nothing," I said. "How can I teach anyone anything?" I stood to leave. "I am content raising my sons and teaching young orphans to read. They will learn for themselves."

Plato jumped up and caught my hand. "We don't have to get married. Just be with me. I will take an oath of chastity for you and only you."

I looked past Plato and saw Lamprocles off in the distance. I wanted nothing but to go home.

"Myrto," Plato whispered. "I would never force myself upon you." He turned me so that we were facing the river together. After several moments of silence, he smiled. "I would, however, allow you to seduce me any time you desire."

That smile had once brought warmth to my cheeks and stirring in my chest, but not today. There was none of that. My life was my own, and I would keep it that way. "No," I said softly. "It's time for me to go home."

Plato brushed the grass from his tunic and looked across the river to the wall surrounding Athens. I walked with him up the embankment and over to the bridge. We stood silently on the bridge, staring at our reflections in the water below.

"I'll walk you home," he said.

"No," I replied. "I'll walk back with Lamprocles."

"I'll return tomorrow and ask you again," he said. "And the day after that and the day after that. I'll come back every day until you agree to marry me," he insisted.

"No," I said again. "You will live your life and let me live mine. There is no greater gift we could offer in memory of Socrates than to know and to be ourselves."

Plato's shoulders slumped and his head hung low. When he finally looked up at me I could see tears streaming down his face. "That's it? Can I offer you nothing?"

I could feel the tears on my cheeks as well. I forced a smile. "For me, nothing is the beginning of everything."

Plato shook his head. "You are even more puzzling than Socrates. And now I've lost you both." He kissed me on the cheek and walked sadly across the bridge alone.

I turned and walked back to where Lamprocles was waiting. "You're not going to marry him?" he asked anxiously.

"No," I replied. "I cannot be who he wants me to be."

Lamprocles leaped into the air with a shout. When he landed, he threw his arms around me and hugged me.

"Let's go home," Lamprocles said.

"Yes," I agreed. "Let's go home."

Author's Note

HISTORIANS DISAGREE ON whether or not Socrates married Myrto. Of those who believe he did, some say that Myrto was Socrates' first wife and that Xanthippe was Socrates' second wife and the mother of all three of his sons. Others say that Myrto was Socrates' second wife and the mother of his two youngest sons.

Most of what we know about Socrates comes from his student, Plato. Plato names only Xanthippe as Socrates' wife. Nevertheless, Plato's student Aristotle wrote that Socrates married Xanthippe first, and that she was the mother of Lamprocles. Later, Socrates took Myrto, a descendant of Aristides the Just, as his second wife. According to Aristotle, Myrto had no dowry, and was the mother of Sophroniscus and Menexenus. *Just Myrto* implies that Plato wrote Myrto out of history because she did not return his love. While this is pure conjecture by the author, it would be ironic if Myrto's feelings for Plato were in fact "platonic."

Socrates' manner of questioning has become known as the Socratic Method. Plato's Socratic dialogues provide the foundation for western thought, yet the opportunity for eastern influence and mysticism existed as well. The art of self-inquiry inherent in the Socratic Method is a universally spiritual practice.

Acropolis – The ancient fortress of Athens including buildings such as the Parthenon.

Acheron – Known as the river of pain, Acheron was one of the five rivers of the Greek underworld (Hades).

Achilles – A Greek warrior, hero of the Trojan War and central character of Homer's *The Illiad.*

Aeschylus – (c. 525 – 456 BCE) Ancient Greek playwright, often called the father of tragedy.

Aesop – (c. 620–564 BCE) Ancient Greek storyteller credited with writing many fables.

Agora – The gathering place or central market in ancient Greek cities.

Alcaeus – (c. 620 – 6th century BCE) Ancient Greek lyric poet and alleged lover of Sappho.

Alcibiades – (c. 450 – 404 BCE) Famous Athenian statesman, orator and general. Subject of two dialogues by Plato (*Alcibiades I* and *II* 103a – 151c).

Alopeke – Home of Socrates, southeast of the Acropolis.

Amazon – A nation of women warriors in Greek mythology.

Ambrosia – Food or drink of the Greek gods.

Antigone – A tragedy written by Sophocles circa 441 BCE; in Greek mythology, Antigone was the daughter of Oedipus and Jocasta (mother of Oedipus).

Anytus – One of the Athenian politicians who prosecuted Socrates (*Apology* 23e).

Aphrodite – Greek goddess of love and procreation.

Apollo – Greek god of the sun, god of the Oracle at Delphi, and twin brother of goddess Artemis.

Ares – Greek god of war.

Aristides – Grandson of Aristides the Just, son of Lysimachus, student of Socrates (*Laches* 179b, *Theages* 130a).

Aristides the Just – (c. 530 – 468 BCE) Athenian statesman and general. son of Lysimachus, father of Lysimachus, grandfather of Aristides, and grandfather or ancestor of Myrto.

Aristocles – Plato's given name at birth.

Ariston – Plato's father.

Aristophanes – (c. 446 - 386 BCE) A comic playwright of ancient Athens whose surviving plays include *The Acharnians* (unflattering to Aspasia) and *The Clouds* (unflattering to Socrates).

Artemis – Greek goddess of hunting and childbirth, protector of young girls; often represented by the moon, Artemis is the twin sister of god Apollo.

Asclepius – Greek god of medicine and healing.

Aspasia – (c. 470 - 400 BCE) Foreign wife of the Athenian statesman Pericles, teacher of Socrates (*Menexenus* 235e – 249e).

Athena – Greek goddess of wisdom and justice; also known as sometimes called Pallas Athena.

Athens – Powerful city-state in ancient Greece.

Chaos – The dark, silent abyss from which all things came into existence; formless matter.

Chaerophon – (c. 465 – 401 BCE) Friend of Socrates who asked the Oracle at Delphi if anyone was wiser than Socrates (*Apology* 21a).

Charmides – (c. 450 – 403 BCE) Plato's uncle; one of the Thirty Tyrants.

Chorus – In classical Greek plays, this group of performers acted as a collective voice for dramatic action, providing background and other crucial information.

Colonus – In ancient Greece, a town just northwest of Athens; birthplace of Sophocles; burial place of Oedipus.

Connus – Socrates' music teacher (*Menexenus* 236a).

Corinth – A city-state in ancient Greece, roughly halfway between Athens and Sparta.

Creon – Mythological ruler of Thebes; a main character in Sophocles plays *Antigone* and *Oedipus at Colonus*.

Critias – (460 – 403 BCE) Relative of Plato; one of the Thirty Tyrants.

Crito – Socrates' wealthy friend who wants Socrates to escape from prison and go into exile. Subject of a dialogue by Plato (*Crito* 43a – 54e).

Croesus – King of Lydia from 560 - 547 BCE until his defeat by the Persians.

Delium – Site of a battle in the Peloponnesian War in 424 BCE where Alcibiades marched with Socrates after the Athenians were defeated. (*Symposium* 221a-c).

Delos – Island in ancient Greece where the Athenians sent an annual tribute to Apollo. No prisoners could be executed during the ships voyage, so Socrates' execution was delayed until the ship returned.

Demeter – Greek goddess of the harvest; mother of Persephone.

Democritus – (c. 460 – 370 BCE) One of the two founders of ancient theory on atoms; author of *Little Cosmology;* student of Leucippus.

Dionysus – Greek god of wine and the arts.

Ephebe – A young man, aged 18-20, in training to become a good citizen and soldier.

Eros – Greek god of sexual love.

Euripides – (c. 480 – 406 BCE) Ancient Greek playwright.

Eurydice – Creon's wife in Greek mythology and in Sophocles' plays *Antigone* and *Oedipus at Colonus*.

Euthyphro – Young man who brought marcher charges against his father for the death of a servant. Subject of a dialogue by Plato (*Euthyphro* 2a – 16a).

Gorgias – (c. 485 – 380 BCE) A pre-Socratic philosopher, master of rhetoric, and sophist. Subject of a dialogue by Plato (*Gorgias* 447a – 527 e).

Graces – In Greek mythology, three goddesses of charm, beauty, and creativity; Socrates sculpted a statue of the Graces that stood at the entrance to the Acropolis.

Hades – Greek god of death; also the name of the underworld where the dead reside.

Haemon – The son of Creon and Eurydice and lover of Antigone in Sophocles' play *Antigone*.

Helen of Troy – Wife of Menelaus, Helen was considered to be the most beautiful woman in the world. Her abduction by Paris started the Trojan War.

Hera – Greek goddess of marriage; wife of Zeus.

Heraclitus – (c. 535 – 475 BCE) Pre-Socratic Greek philosopher famous for saying, "No man ever steps in the same river twice"; author of *On Nature*.

Hercules – Greek demi-god famous for his strength and adventures.

Hermes – Greek god who acts as messenger and intercessor between mortals and the divine.

Hesiod – (c. 750 – 650 BCE) Ancient Greek poet, author of *Theogony*.

Hestia – Greek goddess of the hearth and domestic life.

Hippocrates – (c. 460 – 370 BCE) Ancient Greek physician credited with coining the Hippocratic Oath.

Homer – (7th or 8th century BCE) Ancient Greek epic poet, author of *The Iliad* and *The Odyssey*.

Hoplite – Citizen soldier of Ancient Greece who wore a suit of armor and fought with bronze spears and shields.

Hygeia – Greek goddess of health and cleanliness.

Hymen – Greek god of marriage ceremonies, inspiring feasts and song.

Hymenaeus – Greek lyric poems sung during the procession of the bride to the groom's house.

Iaso – Greek goddess of recuperation from illness.

The Illiad – Ancient Greek epic poem by Homer about the Trojan War.

Illisus – In ancient Greece, a river just outside the defensive walls of Athens.

Isles of the Blessed – In Greek mythology, a place like paradise where heroes and favored mortals are received by the gods.

Jocasta – In Greek mythology and in Sophocles' play *Oedipus the King*, Jocasta is the mother who abandons Oedipus at birth and later unwittingly becomes his wife.

Lamprocles – Eldest son of Socrates and Xanthippe.

Leon from Salamis – An honorable man unjustly put to death by the Thirty Tyrants. Socrates refused to participate in the injustice (*Apology* 32c-d).

Leucippus – One of the two founders of ancient theory on atoms; author of *Big Cosmology;* Democritus' teacher.

Lycon – A prosecutor in the trial of Socrates (*Apology* 36b).

Lysicles – (c. 478 -428 BCE) Athenian general; Aspasia's husband after Pericles died.

Lysimachus – Son of Aristides the Just (*Laches* 179b, *Theages* 130a).

Medusa – In Greek mythology, a monster with a woman's face and serpent hair; anyone who looked directly at her would turn to stone.

Meletus – Chief prosecutor of Socrates (*Euthyphro* 2b)

Menexenus – Socrates' youngest son, still an infant at the time of Socrates' death; multiple sources (Diogenes Laertius, Athenaeus, Plutarch, Aristotle) suggest that Myrto rather than Xanthippe was Menexenus' mother.

Mount Olympus – Home of the twelve Olympian gods.

Muses – Eight Greek goddesses of inspiration for literature, the arts and science; Plato names the poet Sappho as the ninth muse. (*Epigrams* 16).

Myrto – (5th century BCE) A descendent, probably the granddaughter, of Aristides the Just; Aristotle and others have named her as Socrates' second wife and the mother of his two youngest sons, Sophroniscus and Menexenus.

Obol – A silver coin in ancient Greece placed in the mouth of the dead to ensure safe passage to the afterlife. Six obols equaled a drachma, which was approximately one day's wage. Those serving on Socrates' jury would have received three obols each.

Odysseus – King of Ithaca and hero of Homer's epic poem *The Odyssey*. Odysseus was also the mastermind behind the Trojan Horse in Homer's *The Illiad*.

The Odyssey – Ancient Greek epic poem by Homer about Odyssey's journey home from the Trojan War.

Oedipus the King – Ancient Greek tragedy by Sophocles first performed in Athens circa 429 BCE. Oedipus was destined from birth to murder his father Laius and marry his mother Jocasta.

Oracle at Delphi – Dating back to 1400 BCE, the Oracle of Delphi was the most important shrine in all Greece where people went have their questions about the future answered by the priestess of Apollo.

Panacea – Greek goddess of universal remedy.

Panathenaic Way – Stretching from one of the city gates through the market place towards the Acropolis, passing the Parthenon and stopping at the altar of Athena, the Panathenaic Way marked the path of the annual procession in celebration of Athena's birthday.

Pandora – In Greek mythology, Pandora was the first human woman created by the gods. According to the myth, Pandora's curiosity led her to open a jar releasing all of the evils of humanity into the world.

Parmenides – (early 5th century BCE) One of the most significant pre-Socratic philosophers; author of *On Nature* and subject of a dialogue by Plato (*Parmenides* 126a – 166c).

Parthenon – Temple of the goddess Athena in the Acropolis in Athens.

Pegasus – The divine winged horse in Greek mythology.

Penelope – The faithful wife of Odysseus.

Pericles – (c. 495 – 429 BCE) The most prominent and influential Greek statesman, orator, and general of Athens during the Golden Age between the Persian and Peloponnesian wars.

Persephone – In Greek mythology, Persephone is the daughter of Zeus and Demeter; she was abducted by Hades and became queen of the underworld where she must remain during the winter months, but she returns to earth each spring.

Persia – A great empire east of ancient Greece that invaded Greece three times during the Persian Wars in the 5th century BCE.

Phaenarete – Socrates' mother; a midwife.

Piraeus – The port city of ancient Athens. At one time the two were connected by long walls for security with a stone gate at the harbor.

Plato – (c. 428 – 348 BCE) Socrates' most famous student and Aristotles' teacher. Through his Socratic dialogues, Plato is credited for laying the foundation of western philosophy and science.

Poseidon – Greek god of the sea.

Protagoras – (c. 490 BCE – 420 BCE) A pre-Socratic Greek philosopher and sophist; subject of a dialogue by Plato (*Protagoras* 309a – 362a).

Pythagoras – (c. 570 – 495 BCE) Ancient Greek philosopher and mathematician, best known for the Pythagorean Theorum.

Sappho – (c. 620 – 570 BCE) Greek lyric poet; Plato calls her the ninth muse (*Epigrams* 16).

Socrates – (c. 469 – 399 BCE) Ancient Greek philosopher, Plato's teacher; best known for his manner of asking questions or the Socratic Method.

Solon – (c. 638 – 558 BCE) Ancient Greek statesman, lawmaker and poet, often credited with laying the foundation for Athenian democracy.

Sophists – In the second half of the 5th century BCE, the Sophists were intellectuals skilled in rhetoric, experts in debate, and able to persuade or convince others of things regardless of truth. Sophistry is also the subject of a dialogue by Plato (*Sophist* 216a -268d).

Sophocles – (c. 496 – 406 BCE) Ancient Greek playwright who wrote *Oedipus the King, Antigone,* and *Oedipus at Colonus.* Sophocles wrote *Oedipus at Colonus* shortly before his death and his grandson (also called Sophocles) produced it at the Festival of Dionysus in 401 BCE.

Sophroniscus – Socrates' father, believed to be a sculptor or stonemason; also Socrates middle son, still a toddler at the time of Socrates' death; multiple sources (Diogenes Laertius, Athenaeus, Plutarch, Aristotle) suggest that Myrto rather than Xanthippe was Sophroniscus' mother.

Sparta – A dominant military power in ancient Greece; between 431 and 404 BCE, Sparta was the principal enemy of Athens during the Peloponnesian War.

Sphinx – A mythical creature with the body of a lion, wings of an eagle, head of a woman and tail of a serpent that guarded the entrance of Thebes and required travelers to answer a riddle before allowing them to pass.

Styx – A river in Greek mythology that formed the boundary between earth and the underworld.

Thales – (c. 624 BC – 546 BCE) The first Greek philosopher who attempted to explain natural phenomena without reference to mythology; also considered to be the first true mathematician in ancient Greece.

Theano – (6th century BCE) Wife of Pythagoras and author of *Pythagorean Apophthegms, Female Advice, On Virtue, On Piety, On Pythagoras, Philosophical Commentaries,* and *Letters,* but none of her actual writings have survived.

Thebes – Ancient city in central Greece; home to many kings and site of many legends in Greek mythology.

Theogony – A poem by Hesiod composed circa 700 BCE describing the genealogy or birth of the Greek gods.

Theseus – The mythical founder and king of Athens in ancient Greece who slayed the Minotaur; the Athenians sent a religious mission to the island of Delos every year on Theseus's ship in honor of Apollo. No executions were permitted from the time the ship sailed until its return several weeks later.

Thirty Tyrants – The pro-Spartan rulers in Athens after Sparta defeated Athens in the Peloponnesian War in 404 BCE. They were overthrown in 403 BCE.

Trojan Horse – The mythological, huge wooden horse the Greeks used to sneak soldiers into the city of Troy and win the Trojan War.

Trojan War – One of the most important events in Greek mythology made famous through Homer's *The Illiad* and *The Odyssey*. Whether or not the myth is based on any historical reality remains an open question.

Xanthippe – Socrates' wife and the mother of at least one of his three sons; Xanthippe's family may have been more socially prominent than Socrates' family because the ancient Greek custom was to name one's first son after the more illustrious of the two grandfathers, and Socrates' eldest son was named Lamprocles, presumably after Xanthippe's father.

Zeus – Greek god of sky and thunder who rules all the gods and men from Mount Olympus.

Note: References to Plato's work include the "Stephanus numbers" commonly used in scholarly references to the works of Plato to indicate the corresponding page and section of the Greek text as edited by the French scholar Henri Estienne, aka Stephanus in Latin (Paris, 1578).

About the Author

As a teacher and attorney, Laurie Gray has always been a fan of the Ancient Greek philosopher Socrates and the Socratic Method. In addition to writing, speaking and consulting through her company Socratic Parenting LLC, Laurie currently works as a bilingual child forensic interviewer at her local Child Advocacy Center and as an adjunct professor of criminal sciences at Indiana Tech University. She has served on the Faculty at the National Symposium on Child Abuse annually since 2009. Her debut novel *Summer Sanctuary* received a Moonbeam Gold Medal for excellence in young adult fiction and was named an Indiana Best Book Finalist. Laurie is also the author of *Maybe I Will* and *A Simple Guide to Socratic Parenting*. You can visit her online at www.SocraticParenting.com.